Thomas William Robertson

Caste

An Original Comedy in Three Acts

Thomas William Robertson

Caste

An Original Comedy in Three Acts

ISBN/EAN: 9783744786850

Printed in Europe, USA, Canada, Australia, Japan

Cover: Foto ©Andreas Hilbeck / pixelio.de

More available books at **www.hansebooks.com**

CASTE.

CAST OF CHARACTERS.

	Prince of Wales' Theatre, London, April 6, 1867.	Broadway Theatre, New York, August 5, 1867.
Hon. George D'Alroy	Mr. Fred Younge,	Mr. W. J. Florence.
Captain Hawtree	Mr. Sidney Bancroft,	Mr. Owen Marlowe.
Eccles	Mr. George Honey,	Mr. Wm. Davidge.
Samuel Gerridge Dixon	Mr. John Hare,	Mr. Edward Lamb.
Marquise de St. Maur	Miss Sophia Larkin,	Mrs. G. H. Gilbert.
Polly Eccles	Miss Marie Wilton,	Mrs. W. J. Florence.
Esther Eccles	Miss Lydia Foote,	Mrs. S. F. Chanfrau.

Act I.—The little House in Stangate.———COURTSHIP.
Act II.—A Lodging in Mayfair.————MATRIMONY.
Act III.—The little House in Stangate.——WIDOWHOOD.

A lapse of eight months occurs between the first and second Acts, and a lapse of twelve months between the second and third.

Time of performance.—Two hours and forty-five minutes.

THE ARGUMENT.

Hon. George D'Alroy, a rich and aristocratic army officer, falls desperately in love with Esther Eccles, an amiable and good girl, poor and

CASTE

AN ORIGINAL COMEDY IN THREE ACTS

BY

T. W. ROBERTSON

New American Edition, Correctly Reprinted from the
Original Authorized Acting Edition, with the Original
Casts of the Characters, Argument of the Play,
Time of Representation, Description of the
Costumes, Scene and Property Plots, Dia-
grams of the Stage Settings, Sides of
Entrance and Exit, Relative Posi-
tions of the Performers, Expla-
nation of the Stage Direc-
tions, etc., and all of
the Stage Business.

NEW YORK

HAROLD ROORBACH

PUBLISHER

of humble station, who, with her sister POLLY, works hard to support a drunken father not caring how he gets money so long as he does not work for it. Mindful of the stern decrees of CASTE, D'ALROY has tried to dispel his infatuation by various means, but to no purpose; finally he turns for advice to his friend CAPTAIN HAWTREE, who, being a man of the world, counsels anything but marriage, in view of the social gulf between the lovers, and subsequently runs afoul of MR. SAM GERRIDGE, POLLY's sweetheart and something in the mechanical line. But in spite of their difference in station, in spite of the dictates of reason, in spite of the world, D'ALROY declares himself to ESTHER and is accepted.

Six months later finds the pair happily married and quartered in lodgings, without the knowledge of D'ALROY's mother, the MARQUISE OF ST. MAUR, whom he has not informed of his marriage, fearing to incur her displeasure. Meanwhile D'ALROY has been ordered off to India, on active service with his regiment, but can not bring himself to break the news to his wife. While devising some means of disclosing the unwelcome tidings, he is surprised by a visit from his mother, who comes to bid him adieu and urge him to distinguish himself as becomes his birth and position. ESTHER overhears this conversation from an adjoining room and is overwhelmed at the prospect of her husband's departure. This precipitates the truth about D'ALROY's *mésalliance*, to the horror of the MARQUISE, whose disgust is heightened by the appearance of POLLY, SAM and old ECCLES, each of whom is presented in turn, and the high born lady expresses her contempt in no uncertain terms. The time for departure having arrived, D'ALROY goes off with HAWTREE, after comforting his wife as best he can, and leaving suitable provision for her maintenance during his absence.

One year after, ESTHER, with her child, is back in her old home, her husband reported captured and killed by the Sepoys and her money squandered by old ECCLES. Too proud to appeal to the MARQUISE for aid, though urged so to do by HAWTREE, who has returned and proved his friendship in many ways, she is stung by insulting offers of charity from her husband's mother who has learned of her situation through a begging letter privately sent by ECCLES. While at supper, POLLY, SAM and HAWTREE are thunderstruck at the apparition of D'ALROY, the report of whose death proves untrue. The joyful news is broken gently to ESTHER, and an affecting reunion ensues between husband and wife. The MARQUISE, overjoyed at her son's restoration, becomes willingly reconciled to her new daughter; ECCLES is comfortably disposed of by HAWTREE, whose *fiancée* has jilted him for a man of higher rank; POLLY and SAM purchase the fixtures and good will of the late Binks, plumber, and a climax of happiness is reached, despite the inexorable laws of CASTE.

COSTUMES.

GEORGE D'ALROY.—*Act I;* Black coat and vest, gray trousers with black seam, derby hat. *Act II;* British officer's uniform, blue, dead gold cord to trousers, spurs. *Act III;* Black suit, short skirted coat, low crowned black hat. Carries watch throughout.

HAWTREE.—*Act I;* Like D'ALROY. *Act II;* Like D'ALROY, sword on. *Act III;* Black walking suit. Watch.

ECCLES.—*Acts I* and *II;* Shabby black suit, dusty shoes, battered black hat, black necktie. *Act III;* Same, but more shabby.

SAM GERRIDGE.—*Acts I* and *III;* White jacket, red vest, gray trousers, cap. *Act II;* "Sunday clothes,"—flashy and cheap.

DIXON.—Black valet's suit, white necktie.

MARQUISE.—*Act II;* Handsome walking dress. *Act III;* Fashionable mourning.

POLLY.—*Act I;* Bonnet and shawl, light dress, collar and cuffs. *Act II;* Walking dress, hat, parasol. *Act III; 1st,* Black dress, collar and cuffs; *2nd,* change to light dress.

ESTHER.—*Act I;* Costume like POLLY's in same act. *Act II;* Light morning house dress, jewelry, hair fashionably arranged. *Act III;* Full mourning, widow's cap and bands, bonnet to enter with.

STAGE SETTINGS.

Acts I and III.

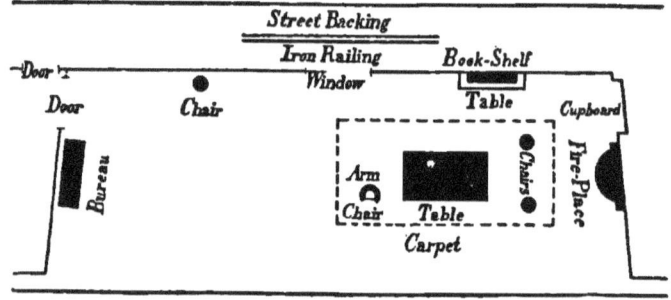

Act II.

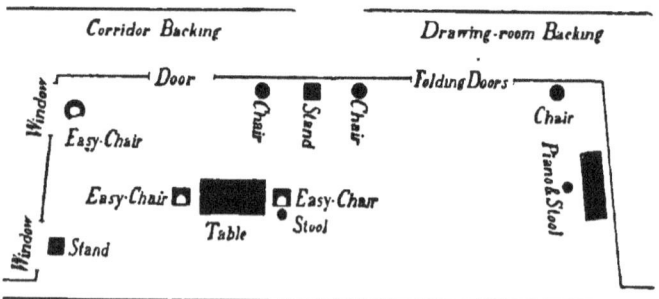

SCENE PLOT.

ACT I.—A plain chamber set in 3 G. Street backing in 4 G. Iron railing, between backing and flat, low enough to get over from the outside.

A window C., in flat, with practical blind. Practical door R. 3 E., which, when opened, shows street door in flat. Mantel and fire-place L. 2 E., two-hinged gas-burners on each side of mantel. Cupboard in recess, L. 3 E. Long table L. C., before fire. Small carpet down. Book shelf against flat, L., under which is a small table. Bureau, R. 2 E. Arm chair R. of table L. C., and two chairs L. of it. Chair up R., near window.

ACT II.—Fancy chamber set in 3 G. Backing in 4 G., representing a drawing-room at the L., and corridor at the R. In flat, practical folding doors L., opening upon drawing-room, and door R., opening upon corridor. Windows, with muslin curtains, R. I E. and R. 3 E. Stand in lower window and small easy chair before upper window. Piano and stool, L. Table R. C., easy chairs R. and L. of it. Foot-stool before L. easy chair. Stand C., against flat, with chair on each side of it. Chair up L.

ACT III.—Same as in Act I, except that piano is in place of bureau, R.; map of India hangs in place of mirror over mantel; cradle up C.

PROPERTIES.

ACT I.—Cane, cigars in case, and eyeglass for HAWTREE. Coin for D'ALROY. Three letters for ESTHER to enter with. Ham, in slices, in paper for POLLY. Foot-rule in SAM'S pocket. Key. Fire, to light. Knives, plates, etc., for setting table. Letter to be handed in at C. window. Tea things, tea pot, tea caddy, tea tray, etc., in cupboard. Books on shelf, and bunch of benefit bills hanging beneath it. Ballet shoes and skirt on small table up L. A few framed theatrical printed portraits and common engravings on walls. Clock, ornaments and matches on mantel. Glass over mantel. Kettle on hob. Small carpet down. Mats inside and outside door R. Furniture as per scene plot.

ACT II.—Curtains at windows. On table, R. C., desert, claret in decanter, two wine glasses half filled, box of cigarettes, vase of flowers, embroidered slippers on canvas, and small basket of colored wools. Ornamental gilt work-basket on stand before window R. I E. Vase of flowers on stand C. Pictures on walls, R., L. and C. Swords and belts for HAWTREE and D'ALROY. Parasol for POLLY. Cigar for SAM. Bottle of Brandy for ECCLES (in call). Eyeglass for MARQUISE. Carpet down. Furniture as per scene plot.

ACT III.—A new table and easy chair for SAM to bring on. Circulars, samples of wall paper, coin, foot-rule and wedding ring for SAM. Pipe, tobacco and bottle for ECCLES. Milk can for D'ALROY to bring on, ready R. U. E. Small box for MARQUISE to bring on at her second entrance. Paper parcels for ESTHER to enter with. Eyeglass and cane for HAWTREE. Letter enclosing a cheque. Milk pitcher, teapot and dishes. Bottle on mantel. Roll of music, tied up, on piano. Map of India, sword embellished with crape knot, spurs and craped cap to hang over mantel. Child, with coral necklace, in cradle. POLLY'S bonnet and shawl hanging on peg, R., on flat. Fire lighted, and kettle on it. Poker at fire. Small tin saucepan on fender. Two candles, in candlesticks, in cupboard. On table, L. C., a slate and pencil, band-box and a ballet skirt.

STAGE DIRECTIONS.

In observing, the player is supposed to face the audience. R., means right; L., left; C., centre; R. C., right of centre; L. C., left of centre; D. F., door in the flat or scene running across the back of the stage; R. F., right side of the flat; L. F., left side of the flat; R. D., right door; L. D., left door; C. D., centre door; I E., first entrance; 2 E., second entrance; U. E., upper entrance; I, 2 or 3 G., first, second or third grooves; UP STAGE, towards the back; DOWN STAGE, towards the audience.

R.   R. C.   C.   L. C.   L.

NOTE.—The text of this play is correctly reprinted from the original authorized acting edition, without change. The introduction has been carefully prepared by an expert, and is the only part of this book protected by copyright.

CASTE.

ACT I.

Scene.—*Interior of* ECCLES' *house at Stangate—rapping heard at door,* R., *the handle is then shaken as curtain rises—the door is unlocked*—enter GEORGE *and* HAWTREE.

Geo. I told you so, the key was left under the mat in case I came. They're not back from rehearsal. (*crosses,* C., *to fireplace*)

Haw. (*looking round*) And this is the Fairy's Bower.

Geo. And this is the Fairy's fireplace ; the fire is laid, I'll light it. (*lights fire with lucifer from mantelpiece*)

Haw. And this is the abode rendered blessed by her abiding. It is here that she dwells, walks, talks, eats and drinks. Does she eat and drink ?

Geo. Yes, heartily. I've seen her.

Haw. And you are really spoons—case of true love—hit dead.

Geo. Right through. Can't live away from her. (*with elbow on other end of mantel up stage*)

Haw. Poor old Dal! And you've brought me over the water to——

Geo. Stangate.

Haw. Stangate—to see her for the same sort of reason that when a patient is in a dangerous state one doctor calls in another for a consultation.

Geo. Yes! Then the patient dies.

Haw. Tell us all about it. You know I've been away. (*sits right of table, leg on chair*)

Geo. Well, then, eighteen months ago——

Haw. Oh, cut that. You told me all about that. You went to the theatre and saw a girl in a ballet, and you fell in love.

Geo. Yes, I found out that she was an amiable good girl.

Haw. Of course. Cut that. We'll credit her with all the virtues and accomplishments.

Geo. Who worked hard to support a drunken father.

Haw. Oh, the father's a drunkard, is he? The father doesn't inherit the daughter's virtues.

Geo. No, I hate him.

Haw. Naturally, quite so, quite so.

Geo. And she, that is Esther, is very good to her younger sister.

Haw. The younger sister also angelic, amiable, accomplished, etc., etc.

Geo. Um, good enough, but got a temper, large temper! Well, with some difficulty I got to speak to her—I mean to Esther ; then I was allowed to see her to her door here.

Haw. I know—pastry-cooks, Richmond dinner, and all that.

Geo. You're too fast. Pastry-cooks, yes—Richmond, no. Your knowledge of the world fifty yards round barracks misleads you. I saw her nearly every day, and I kept on falling in love, falling and falling, till I thought I should never reach the bottom. Then I met you.

Haw. I remember *the* night when you told me, but I knew it was only an amourette. However, if the fire is a conflagration, subdue it ; try dissipation.

Geo. I have.

Haw. What success?

Geo. None. Dissipation brought on bad health, and self-contempt, a sick head and a sore heart.

Haw. Foreign travel. Absence makes the heart grow stronger. Get leave and cut away.

Geo. I did get leave and I did cut away, and while away I was miserable, and a gone 'er coon than ever.

Haw. What's to be done?

Geo. Don't know. That's the reason I asked you to come over and see.

Haw. Of course, Dal, you're not such a soft as to think of marriage. You know what your mother is. Either you are going to behave properly, with a proper regard to the world, and all that, you know, or you're going to do the other thing. Now the question is, what do you mean to do? The girl is a nice girl no doubt, but as to your making her Mrs. D'Alroy the thing is out of the question.

Geo. Why, what should prevent me?

Haw. Caste! The inexorable law of caste. The social law, so becoming and so good, that commands like to mate with like, and forbids a giraffe to fall in love with a squirrel ; that holds sentiment to be a dissipation, and demands the exercise of common sense from all.

Geo. But, my dear Bark——

Haw. My dear Dal, all those marriages of people with common people are all very well in novels and in plays on the stage, because the real people don't exist, and have no relatives who exist, and no connections, and so no harm's done, and it's rather interesting to look at ; but in real life, with real relations, and real mothers, and so forth, it's absolute bosh—it's worse ; its utter social and personal annihilation and individual damnation.

Geo. As to my mother, I havn't thought about her.

Haw. Of course not. Lovers are so damned selfish they never think of anybody but themselves.

Geo. My father died when I was three years old, and she married again before I was six, and married a Frenchman.

Haw. A nobleman of the most ancient families in France, of equal blood to her own ; she obeyed the duties imposed upon her by her station, and by caste.

Geo. Still it caused a separation and a division between us, and I never see my brother because he lives abroad. Of course the Marquise de St. Maur is my mother, and I look upon her with a sort of superstitious awe.

Haw. She's a grand Brahmin priestess.

Geo. Just so, and I know I'm a fool ; and my having a thick tongue and lisping makes me seem more foolish than I am. Now you're clever, Bark, a little too clever, I think. You're paying your devoirs, that's the correct word I think—to Lady Florence Carburry, the daughter of a Countess—she's above you, you've no title. Is she to forget *her* caste?

Haw. That argument doesn't apply ; a man can be no more than a gentleman.

Geo. " Kind hearts are more than coronets and simple faith than Norman blood."

Haw. Now, George, if you're going to consider this question from a point of view of poetry, you're off to no man's land, where I won't follow you.

Geo. No gentleman can be ashamed of the woman he loves, no matter what her original station—once his wife he raises her to his rank.

Haw. Yes, he raises her—her—but her connections—her relatives. How about them ?

Enter, ECCLES, D. R.

Ecc. (entering) Polly !—Why the devil !—(*seeing them assumes a deferential manner*) Oh, Mr. De Alroy, I didn't see you, sir. Good afternoon—the same to you, sir, and many on 'em. (*down, R.*)

Geo. (*who has come down C., crosses to* HAWTREE) This is papa.

Haw. Ah! (*leaning on corner of mantelpiece and scanning* ECCLES *through eye-glass*)

Geo. Miss Eccles and her sister not returned from rehearsal yet?

Ecc. No, sir, they have not ; I expect 'em in directly. I hope you've been quite well since I saw you last, sir ?

Geo. Quite, thank you ; and how have you been, Mr. Eccles?

Ecc. Well, sir, I have not been the thing at all. My 'ealth, sir, and my spirits is both broken. I am not the man I used to be—I am not accustomed to this sort of thing. I have seen better days —but they are gone, most like for ever. It's a melancholy thing, sir, for a man of my time of life to look back on better days that are gone most like for ever.

Geo. I daresay.

Ecc. Once proud and prosperous, I am now poor and lowly— once master of a shop, I am now, by the pressure of circumstances over which I have no control, driven to seek work and not find it. Poverty is a dreadful thing, sir, for a man as had once been well off.

Geo. I daresay.

Ecc. (*sighing*) Ah! sir, the poor and lowly is often hardly used. What chance has the working man?

Haw. None. (*aside*) When he don't work.

Ecc. We are all equal in mind and feeling.

Haw. I hope not.

Ecc. I am sorry, gentlemen, that I cannot offer you any refresh-ment, but luxury and me has long been strangers.

Geo. (*taking* ECCLES *aside from* HAWTREE) I am very sorry for your misfortunes, Mr. Eccles. May I hope that you will allow me to offer you this trifling loan ? (*giving him half-a-sovereign*)

Ecc. Sir, you are a gentleman—one can tell a real gentleman, sir, with half-a-sov—I mean with half a eye—a real gentleman, and understand the natural emotions of the working man. Pride, sir, is a thing as should be put down by the strong, and of pecu-niary necessity. I promised a friend to meet him at this time in the neighborhood, on a matter of business—so if you'll excuse me, sir.

Geo. With pleasure.

Ecc. (*going, up* R.) Sorry to leave you, gentlemen—but——

Geo. Don't stay on my account.

Haw. Don't mention it.

Ecc. Business is business. (*goes up*, D. R.) The girls will be here directly. Good afternoon, gentlemen.   **Exit,** D. R.

Geo. (*sighing*) Ah !

Haw. The papa is not nice, but " Kind hearts are more than coronets, and simple faith than Norman blood." Poor George ! I wonder what your mamma, the most noble the Marquise de St. Maur, would think of Papa Eccles. Come, Dal, allow that there is something in caste. Conceive that dirty ruffian, that rinsing of stale beer, that walking tap-room, for a father-in-law. Go out in Central America. Forget her.

Geo. Can't.

Haw. You'll be wretched and miserable with her.

Geo. I'd rather be wretched with her than miserable without her. (HAWTREE *takes out cigar case*) Don't smoke here.

Haw. Why not?

Geo. She'll be coming in directly.

Haw. I don't think she'd mind.

Geo. I should ; do you smoke before Lady Florence Carburry?

Haw. (*closing case*) Ha! you're suffering from a fit of the morals.

Geo. What is that?

Haw. The morals is a disease, like the measles, that attacks the young and innocent.

Geo. (*with temper*) You talk like Mephistophiles without the cleverness. (*goes up to window and looks at watch*)

Haw. (*crosses*) I don't pretend to be a particularly good sort of fellow, nor a particularly bad sort of fellow. I suppose I'm about the average standard sort of thing, and I don't like to see a friend go down hill to the devil while I can put the drag on. (*turning with back to fire*) Here is a girl of humble station, poor, and all that, with a drunken father, who evidently doesn't care how he gets money so long as he doesn't work for it. Marriage—pah! Couldn't the thing be arranged? (*goes up again*)

Geo. Hawtree, cut that. (*at window*) She's here. (*turns from window*—enter, ESTHER, D. R —GEORGE *receives her at door; flurried at sight of her*) Good morning, I got here before you, you see.

Est. Good morning.

Geo. I've taken the liberty—I hope you won't be angry—of asking you to let me present a friend of mine to you. Miss Eccles, Captain Hawtree.

HAWTREE *advances and bows*—GEORGE *assists* ESTHER *in taking off bonnet and shawl.*

Haw. (*aside*) Pretty.

Est. (*aside*) Thinks too much of himself.

Geo. You've had a late rehearsal. Where's Polly ?

Est. She stayed behind to buy something.

Enter, POLLY, D. R.—*these two girls to be dressed alike—ballet girl's kiss-me-quick curls, &c.*

Pol. Hallo, Mr. D'Alroy, how de do? Ah, I am tired to death. Kept at rehearsal by an old fool of a stage manager—but stage managers are always old fools—except when they're young ones. We shan't have time for any dinner, so I've brought something for tea, ham. (*showing ham in paper, and seeing* HAWTREE) Oh, I beg your pardon, sir, I didn't see you.

Geo. A friend of mine, Mary, Captain Hawtree. Miss Mary Eccles. (*crosses*)

Pol. (*aside*) What a swell! Got nice teeth, and he knows it. (*takes off bonnet and shawl*) How quiet we all are. Let's talk about something. (*she crosses to fire,* L., *round table-front*—HAWTREE *comes round to* R. *of table*)

Est. What can we talk about?

Pol. Anything. (*puts ham from paper on to plate*) Ham, Mr. D'Alroy? Do you like ham?

Geo. I adore her. (*crosses*) I mean I adore it.

Pol. (*to* HAWTREE) Do you like ham, sir?

Haw. Yes.

Pol. Now that is very strange. I should have thought you'd have been above ham.

Haw. Why? May I ask why?

Pol. You look above it. You look quite equal to tongue-glazed. (*laughing*) Mr. D'Alroy is here so often that he knows our ways.

Haw. I like everything that is piquante and fresh, and pretty, and agreeable.

Pol. Ah! you mean that for me. (*curtseying*) Oh! (*sings*) Tra, la lal la la! Now I must put the kettle on. (GEORGE *and* ESTHER *are at window*) Esther never does any work when Mr. D'Alroy is here. They're spooning. Ugly word, spoon, isn't it? Reminds me of red currant jam. By-the-bye, love is very like currant jam—at the first taste, sweet; afterwards shuddery. Do you ever spoon?

Haw. I should like to do so at this moment.

Pol. No, you're too grand for me. There's too much of you for me. You want taking down a peg—I mean a foot. Let's see, what are you, a corporal?

Haw. Captain.

Pol. I prefer corporal. See here, let's change about. You be corporal—it'll do you good—and I'll be my lady.

Haw. Pleasure.

Pol. You must call me my lady, though, or you shan't have any ham.

Haw. Certainly, my lady. But I cannot accept your hospitality, for I'm engaged to dine.

Pol. At what time?

Haw. Seven.

Pol. Seven! Why that's half-past tea time. Now, Corporal, you must wait on me.

Haw. As the pages did of old.

Pol. My lady !

Haw. My lady.

Pol. Here's the kettle, Corporal, take it into the back kitchen. (*crosses*)

Haw. Eh !

Pol. I'm coming too.

Haw. Oh, that alters the case. (*he takes kettle handle between finger and thumb*)

Geo. What are you about ?

Haw. About to fill the kettle. (*holding it out at arm's length*)

Est. (*to* POLLY) Mind what you are doing, Polly ; what will Sam say ?

Pol. Whatever Sam chooses. What the sweetheart don't see the husband can't grieve at. Corporal !

Haw. My lady.

Pol. Forward, march, and mind the soot don't drop upon your trousers.

Exeunt, POLLY *and* HAWTREE, *door,* R.

Est. (*rising*) What a girl it is—all spirits. The worst is that it is so easy to mistake her.

Geo. And so easy to find out your mistake. (*they cross to* L. *down stage*) But why won't you let me present you with a piano? (*following* ESTHER)

Est. I don't want one.

Geo. You said you were fond of playing.

Est. We may be fond of many things without having them. (*crosses, taking out letter*) Now here is a gentleman says that he is attached to me.

Geo. (*jealous*) May I know his name?

Est. What for ? it would be as useless as his solicitations. (*throws letter into fire*)

Geo. I lit that fire. (GEORGE *crosses to fire*)

Est. Then burn these two—no, not that (*snatching one back*), I must keep that, burn the others. (GEORGE *does so, crosses again*)

Geo. Who is that from ?

Est. Why do you wish to know ?

Geo. Because I love you, and I don't think you love me, and I fear a rival.

Est. You have none !

Geo. I know you have so many admirers.

Est. They're nothing to me.

Geo. None ?

Est. No. They're admirers, but there's not a husband among them.

Geo. Not the writer of that letter?

Est. Oh, I like him very much.

Geo. Oh!

Est. And I am very fond of this.

Geo. Then, Esther, you don't care for me!

Est. Don't I? How do you know?

Geo. Because you won't let me read that letter.

Est. It won't please you if you see it.

Geo. I daresay not. That's just the reason that I want to. You won't?

Est. I will—there! (*giving it to him*)

Geo. (*reads*) "Dear madam."

Est. That's tender, isn't it?

Geo. "The terms are £4. Your dresses to be found for eight weeks certain, and longer if you should suit. (GEORGE *in astonishment*) I cannot close the engagement until the return of my partner. I expect him back to-day, and will write you as soon as I have seen him.—Yours very, &c." Four pounds, find dresses! What does this mean?

Est. It means that they want a Columbine for the pantomime at Manchester, and I think I shall get the engagement.

Geo. Manchester? Then you'll leave London.

Est. I must. You see this little house is on my shoulders, Polly, only eighteen shilings a week and father has been out of work a long, long time. I make the bread here, and it's hard to make sometimes. I've been mistress of this place, and forced to think ever since my mother died, and I was eight years old—Four pounds a week is a large sum. I can save out of it.

Geo. But you'll go away and I shan't see you.

Est. Perhaps it will be for the best. What future is there for us? You're a man of rank, and I am a poor girl who gets her living by dancing. It would have been better that we had never met.

Geo. No!

Est. Yes, it would, for I'm afraid that——

Geo. You love me?

Est. I don't know. I'm not sure, but I think I do.

Geo. (*trying to seize her hand*) Esther!

Est. No. Think of the difference of our stations.

Geo. That's what Hawtree says. Caste, caste, curse caste! (*goes up a little*)

Est. If I go to Manchester it will be for the best. We must both try to forget each other.

Geo. Forget you. No, Esther, let me——(*seizing her hand*)

Pol. (*without*) Mind what you are about. Oh dear, oh dear!
(GEORGE *and* ESTHER *retire up* C.)

Enter, POLLY *and* HAWTREE, D. R.

Pol. You nasty great clumsy corporal, you've spilt the water all over my frock. Oh, dear me! (*coming down,* C.)

Haw. Allow me to offer you a new one.

Pol. No, (*takes chair*) I won't. You'll be calling to see how it looks when it's on. Haven't you got a handkerchief? Wipe it dry. (HAWTREE *bends almost on one knee, and wipes dress on her,* L.—enter, SAM, *door* R.)

Sam. Afternoon. (*savagely*) I suppose you didn't hear me knock. The door was open. I'm afraid I intrude.

Pol. No, you don't, we're glad to see you; if you've got a handkerchief help to wipe it dry. (SAM *assists* HAWTREE)

Haw. I'm very sorry. (*rising*)

Pol. It won't spoil it.

Sam. The stain won't come out. (*rising*)

Pol. It's only water.

Sam. Good afternoon, Miss Eccles. (POLLY *rises*) Who's the other swell? (*to* POLLY)

Pol. I'll introduce you. Captain Hawtree—Mr. Sam Gerridge.

Haw. Charmed. (*crosses*) Who's this? (*to* GEORGE *going up*)

Geo. Polly's sweetheart.

Haw. Oh. Now if I can be of no further assistance, I'll go. (*looking at watch*) George, will you? (GEORGE *takes no notice*) Will you?

Geo. What?

Haw. Go with me.

Geo. Go! No.

Haw. (*to* POLLY, *coming down*) Then, Miss Eccles—I mean, my lady. (*shaking hands*)

Pol. (R. C.) Good-bye, Corporal.

Haw. (R. C.) Good-bye. Good afternoon, Mr.——pardon me. (*to* GERRIDGE)

Sam. (*with constrained rage*) Gerridge, sir.

Haw. Ah, Gerridge. Good day. (*going up*)

Exit HAWTREE, D. R.

Sam. Who's that fool? (*to* POLLY) Who's that long idiot?

Pol. I told you—Captain Hawtree.

Sam. What's he want here?

Pol. He's a friend of Mr. D'Alroy's.

Sam. Ugh! Isn't one of 'em enough!

Pol. What do you mean?

Sam. For the neighbors to talk about. Who's he after?

Pol. What do you mean by after? You're forgetting yourself, I think.

Sam. No I'm not forgetting myself—I'm remembering you. What can a long fool of a swell dressed up to the nines within an inch of his life want after two girls of your class. Look at the difference of your stations. They don't come here after any good.

During this speech ESTHER *crosses to fire and sits before it in low chair—*GEORGE *follows her and sits on her* L.

Pol. Samuel!

Sam. I mean what I say. People ought to stick to their own class. Life is a railway journey, and mankind is a passenger—first class, second class, third class. Any person found riding in a superior class to that for which he has taken his ticket will be removed at the first station stopped at, according to the bye-laws of the company.

Pol. You're giving yourself nice airs. What business is it of yours who comes here? Who are you?

Sam. I'm a mechanic.

Pol. That's evident.

Sam. I'm not ashamed of it. I'm not ashamed of my paper cap.

Pol. Why should you be? I daresay Captain Hawtree isn't ashamed of his fourteen and sixpenny gossamer.

Sam. You think a lot of him cos' he's a captain. Why did he call you my lady?

Pol. Because he treated me as one. I wish you'd make the same mistake. (*they bounce up stage wrangling*)

Est. (*sitting with* GEORGE, *tête-a-tête by fire*) But we must listen to reason.

Geo. I hate reason.

Est. I wonder what it means?

Geo. Everything disagreeable. When people insist on talking unpleasantly, they always say listen to reason.

Sam. (*coming down*) What will the neighbors say?

Pol. I don't care. (*coming down*)

Sam. What will the neighbors *think?*

Pol. They'll *think* nothing. They can't think. Like you, they've not been educated up to it.

Sam. It all comes of your being on the stage.

Pol. It all comes of your not understanding me or anything else but putty. Now, if you were a gentleman——

Sam. Then of course I should make up to a lady. (*they bounce up stage again*)

Geo. Reason's an idiot, two and two are four, and twelve and eight are twenty. That's reason.

Sam. (*coming down*) The stage! Painting your cheeks.

Pol. Better paint our *cheeks* than paint *nasty old doors* as you do. How can you understand art? You, a mechanic. You're not a professional; you're not in trade; you are not of the same station that we are. When the manager speaks to you, you touch your hat, and say, " Yes, sir," because he's your superior.

Geo. When people love there's no such thing as money. It don't exist.

Est. Yes, it does.

Geo. Then it oughtn't to.

Sam. The manager employs me, as he does you. Payment is good everywhere and anywhere, whatever is commercial is right.

Pol. Actors are not like mechanics. They wear cloth coats, and not fustian jackets.

Sam. I dislike play-actors.

Pol. And I despise mechanics. (*they tear up stage again*)

Geo. I never think of anything else but you.

Est. Really!

Sam. (*coming down*) Polly, I won't stay here to be insulted. (*putting on cap*)

Pol. Nobody wants you to stay. Go!

Sam. I will go. Good-bye, Miss Mary Eccles. (*crosses C. to door, R.*) I shan't come here again. (*turning to door*)

Pol. Don't! good riddance to bad rubbish!

Sam. You can go to your *captain*.

Pol. And you to your putty. (*leaning against table facing him*)

Est. And so you think you shall always love as you do now?

Geo. More!

Pol. Now, you shan't go. (*locking door, taking out key, which she pockets ; places back against door*) Now I'll just show you my power.

Sam. Miss Eccles, let me out. (*advancing to door*)

Pol. Shan't.

Est. Now you two. (*postman's knock*) The postman.

Sam. Now you must let me go ; you must unlock the door!

Pol. No, I needn't. (*opens window, looking out*) Here, postman. (*takes letter*) Thank you ; Esther.

Est. (*rising*) For me?

Pol. Yes. (*gives it to her, closes window, and returns to door triumphantly*)

Est. (*going down L. of table*) From Manchester.

Geo. Manchester? (*coming down L., back of table*)

Est. (L. C., *reading*) I've got the engagement, £4 a week.
(GEORGE *places his arm round her*)

Geo. You shan't go, Esther. Stay, be my wife.

Est. But the world, your world?

Geo. Damn the world, you're my world. Stay with your husband, Mrs. D'Alroy.

Sam. I *will* go out. (*with sudden determination*)

Pol. You can't and you shan't.

Sam. I can. I will! (*opens window and jumps out*)

Pol. (*frightened*) He's hurt himself. Sam, dear Sam! (*running to window*—SAM'S *face appears at window*—POLLY *shuts it down violently—during this* GEORGE *has kissed* ESTHER)

Geo. My wife! (*the handle of door is heard to rattle, then the door is shaken violently*—ESTHER *crosses to* POLLY, *up* C., *who gives her key*—ESTHER *then opens the door*—ECCLES *reels in very drunk and clings to the corner of bureau,* R., *for support*—GEORGE *stands* L. C., *pulling his moustache*—ESTHER *a little way up* R. C., *looking with shame first at her father, then at* GEORGE—POLLY *sitting in window recess, up* C.

ACT DROP.

For Call.—GEORGE *hat in hand bidding* ESTHER *good-bye,* R., ECCLES *sitting in chair, nods before the fire*—SAM *again looks in at window*—POLLY *pulls the blind violently.*

ACT II.

Scene.—GEORGE's *lodgings in Mayfair, opening on the drawing-room*—ESTHER *and* GEORGE *discovered sitting in easy chairs,* R. *and* L. *of table;* GEORGE *has his uniform trowsers and spurs on.*

Est. George, dear, you seem out of spirits.

Geo. (*smoking cigarette*) Not at all, dear; not at all. (*rallying*)

Est. Then why don't you talk?

Geo. I've nothing to say.

Est. That's no reason.

Geo. I can't talk about nothing.

Est. Yes, you can. You often do. You used to do so before we were married. (*crosses to* GEORGE *and caresses him*)

Geo. No, I didn't. I talked about you and my love for you. D'ye call that nothing?

Est. (*sitting on stool,* L. *of* GEORGE) How long have we been married, dear? Let me see, six months yesterday. (*dreamily*) It hardly seems a week. It almost seems a dream.

Geo. Awfully jolly dream. Don't let us wake up. (*aside*) How ever shall I tell her?

Est. And when I married you I was twenty-two, wasn't I?

Geo. Yes, dear; but then you know you must have been some age or other.

Est. No: but to think that I'd lived two-and-twenty years without knowing you.

Geo. What of it, dear?

Est. It seems such a dreadful waste of time.

Geo. So it was, awful.

Est. Do you remember our first meeting? Then I was in the ballet.

Geo. Yes. Now you're in the heavies.

Est. Then I was in the front rank. Now I'm of high rank. The Hon. Mrs. George D'Alroy. You promoted me to be your wife.

Geo. No, dear. You promoted me to be your husband.

Est. And now I'm one of the aristocracy, ain't I ?

Geo. Yes, dear. I suppose that we may consider ourselves——

Est. Tell me, George, are you quite sure that you are proud of your poor little humble wife ?

Geo. Proud of you ! Proud as the winner of the Derby.

Est. Wouldn't you have loved me better if I'd been a lady ?

Geo. You are a lady. You're Mrs. D'Alroy.

Est. What will your mamma say when she knows of your marriage. I quite tremble at the thought of meeting her.

Geo. So do I. Luckily she's in Rome.

Est. Do you know, George, I should like to be married all over again.

Geo. Not to anybody else, I hope ?

Est. My darling !

Geo. But why over again. Why?

Est. Our courtship was so beautiful ! it was like in a novel from the library, only better. You, a fine, rich, high-born gentleman, coming to our humble little house to court poor me. Do you remember the ballet you first saw me in? that was at Covent Garden. "Jeanne la Folle, or, The Return of the Soldier." (*goes to piano*) Don't you remember the dance? (*plays piano*)

Geo. Esther, how came you to learn to play the piano? Did you teach yourself ?

Est. Yes; so did Polly. We can only just touch the notes, to amuse ourselves.

Geo. How was it ?

Est. I've told you so often !

Geo. Tell me again. (ESTHER *returns to stool at his feet*) I'm like the children, I like to hear what I know already.

Est. Well then, mother died when I was quite young ; I can only just remember her. Polly was an infant, so I had to be Polly's mother. Father, who is a very eccentric man, but a very good one, when you know him (GEORGE'S *jaw drops and he pulls his moustache*), did not take much notice of us, and we got on as well as we could. We used to let the first floor, and a lodger took it— Herr Griffenhaagen. He was a ballet master at the opera. He took a fancy to me, and asked me if I should like to learn to dance and I told him father couldn't afford to pay for my tuition ; and he said that (*imitation*) he didn't want payment, but that he would teach me for nothing ; for he had taken a fancy to me, because I was like a little lady he had known long years ago in de far off land he came from. Then he got us an engagement at the theatre. That is how we first were in the ballet.

Geo. That fellow was a great brick ; I should like to ask him to dinner! What became of him?

Est. I don't know, he left England. (GEORGE *fidgets and looks at watch*) You are very restless, George, what's the matter?

Geo. Nothing.

Est. Are you going out?

Geo. Yes. (*looking at his boots and spurs*) That's the reason I dined in these.

Est. To the barracks?

Geo. Yes.

Est. On duty?

Geo. (*hesitating*) On duty! (*rising*) And of course when a man is a soldier he must go on duty when he's ordered, and when he's ordered, and—and—(*aside*) Why did I ever enter the service?

Est. (*rising and twining her arms round him*) George, if you must go out to your club, go. Don't mind leaving me. (*taking his hand*) Somehow or other, George, these last few days everything seems to have changed with me. I don't know why, sometimes my eyes fill with tears for no reason, and sometimes I feel so happy for no reason. I don't mind being left by myself as I used to do. When you are a few minutes behind time I don't run to the window and watch for you, and turn irritable. Not that I love you less, no! for I love you more ; but often when you are away I don't feel that I am by myself. I never feel alone. (*goes to piano and turns over music*)

Geo. What angels women are ! At least this one is ; I forget all about the others. (*carriage wheels heard off*, R.) If I'd known I could have been so happy, I'd have sold out when I married. (*knock at street door*)

Est. (*standing at table*) That's for us.

Geo. (*at first window*) Hawtree in a hansom! (*aside*) He's come for me. I must tell her sooner or later. (*at door*) Come in, Hawtree.

Enter, HAWTREE in regimentals.

Haw. How do? Hope you're well, Mrs. D'Alroy. (*coming down* R., *places cap on table*) George, are you coming to——

Geo. (R. *coming down with him*, C.) No, I've dined. We've dined early.

ESTHER *plays scraps of music at piano.*

Haw. (*crosses*, R., *sotto voce*) Haven't you told her?
Geo. (*going down* L. *of* HAWTREE) No, I daren't.
Haw. But you must.
Geo. You know what an awful coward I am. You do it for me.
Haw. Not for worlds. I have just had my own adieu to make.
Geo. Ah, yes, to Florence Carburry; how did she take it?
Haw. Oh, very well!
Geo. Did she cry?
Haw. No.
Geo. Nor exhibit any emotion whatever?
Haw. No, not particularly.
Geo. Didn't you kiss her?
Haw. No, Lady Clardonax was in the room.
Geo. Didn't she squeeze your hand?
Haw. No.
Geo. Didn't she say anything?
Haw. No, except that she hoped to see me back again soon, and that India was a bad climate.
Geo. Umph! It seems to have been a tragic parting, almost as tragic as parting your back hair.
Haw. Lady Florence is not the sort of person to make a scene.
Geo. To be sure she's not your wife! I wish Esther would be as cool and comfortable. (*after a pause*) No, I don't. (*a rap at door* —enter DIXON) Oh, Dixon, lay out my——
Dix. I have laid them out; everything is ready.
Geo. (*after a pause*, *irresolutely*) I must tell her, mustn't I?
Haw. Better send for her sister. Let Dixon go for her in a cab.
Geo. Just so. I'll send him at once. Dixon—(*goes up and talks to* DIXON)
Est. (*rising*) Do you want to have a talk with my husband? Shall I go into the dining-room?
Haw. No, Mrs. D'Alroy. (*going to her at piano*)
Geo. No, dear. At once, Dixon. Tell the cabman to drive like—(exit DIXON)—like a cornet just joined. (*going down*, R. C.)
Est. (*to* HAWTREE) Are you going to take him anywhere?
Haw. No. (*aside*) Yes, to India. (*crosses*, C., *to* GEORGE) Tell her now.
Geo. No, no. I'll wait till I put on my uniform. (*going up* R.; *the door opens and* POLLY *peeps in*)
Pol. How d'ye do, good people? quite well?
Geo. Eh! Didn't you meet Dixon?
Pol. Who?
Geo. Dixon—my man.
Pol. No.

Geo. (*crosses*) Confound it ! He'll have his ride for nothing.

Pol. Bless you, my turtles. (*blessing them ballet fashion*) George, kiss your mother. (R. C., *he kisses her*) That's what I call an honorable brother-in-law's kiss. I'm not in the way, am I ?

Geo. (R., *behind easy chair*) Not at all. I'm very glad you've come.

Haw. (*back to audience and elbow on easy chair*, R.; *aside to* GEORGE) Under ordinary circumstances she's not a very eligible visitor.

Geo. Caste again. (*going up*, R.) I'll be back directly.

                                                        Exit GEORGE.

Haw. (*crosses*, L.) Mrs. D'Alroy, I——(*shakes hands*)

Est. (*who is standing over* POLLY, *at piano*) Going ?

Pol. (*rising*) I drive you away, Captain ? (*taking her parasol from table*)

Haw. No.

Pol. Yes, I do, I frighten you. I'm so ugly ; I know I do. You frighten me.

Haw. How so ?

Pol. You're so handsome. (*coming down*, L. C.) Particularly in these clothes, for all the world like an inspector of police.

Est. (*half-aside*) Polly !

Haw. (*aside*) This is a wild sort of thing in sisters-in-law.

Pol. Any news, Captain ?

Haw. (*in a drawling tone*) No. Is there any news with you ?

Pol. Yes. We've got a new piece coming out at our theatre.

Haw. What's it about ?

Pol. (*drawling*) I don't know. (*to* ESTHER) Had him there. (HAWTREE *drops sword impatiently*) Going to kill anybody to-day that you've got your sword on ?

Haw. No.

Pol. I thought not. (*sings*)

> " With a sabre on his brow,
> And a helmet by his side ;
> The soldier sweethearts servant maids,
> And eats cold meat besides." (*laughs*)

Enter, GEORGE, *door* R. F., *in uniform, carrying in his hand his sword, sword belt and cap*—ESTHER *meets him, takes them from him and places them on chair up*, L.., *then comes half down*, L.; GEORGE *goes down*, R. C.

Pol. (*clapping her hands*) Oh, here's a beautiful brother-in-law ! Why didn't you come in on your horse as they do at Astley's ? Gallop in and say : (*imitation*) Soldiers of France, the eyes of Europe are a-looking at you. The Empire has confidence in you, and France expects that every man this day will do his little utmost. The foe is before you—more's the pity—and you are before them—worse luck for you! Forward! Go and get killed, and to those who escape the Emperor will give a little bit of ribbon. Nineteens about! Forward! Gallop! Charge! (*galloping round to* R., *imitating bugle and giving point with parasol; she nearly spears* HAWTREE'S *nose—*HAWTREE *claps his hand upon his sword-hilt; she throws herself into chair laughing, and clapping* HAWTREE'S *cap from table upon her head—all laugh and applaud —carriage wheels heard without*)

Pol. What's that? (*a peal of knocks heard at street door*)

Geo. (*who has hastened to window, up* R.) A carriage. Good heavens, my mother!

Haw. (*at window,* R. I E.) The Marchioness!

Est. (*crosses to* GEORGE.) Oh, George!

Pol. (*crosses to window*) A marchioness! A real live marchioness! Let me look! I never saw a——

Geo. (*forcing her from window*) No, no, no! She doesn't know I'm married. I must break it to her by degrees. What shall I do?

Est. Let me go into the bedroom until——

Haw. Too late. She's on the stairs.

Est. Here then. (*going to doors,* L. F.)

Pol. I want to see a real live march——

GEORGE *lifts her in his arms and places her within folding doors with* ESTHER, *crossing to door,* R. F.; HAWTREE *closes folding doors,* L. F., *as* GEORGE *opens door* R. F., *and admits* MARQUISE.

Geo. (*escorting her down stage,* R.) My dear mother, I saw you getting out of the carriage. (HAWTREE, *up,* L.)

Mar. My dear boy (*kissing his forehead*), I am so glad I got to London before you embarked. (GEORGE *nervous;* HAWTREE *coming down,* L.) Captain Hawtree, I think. How do you do?

Haw. (*crosses in front of table*) Quite well, I thank your ladyship. I trust you are?

Mar. (*sitting in easy chair,* R.) Oh, quite, thanks. Do you still see the Countess and Lady Florence?

Haw. Yes.

Mar. Please remember me to them. (HAWTREE *takes cap from table and places sword under his arm*) Are you going?

Haw. Yaas. I am compelled. (*bows, crosses round back of table; to* GEORGE, *who meets him,* R. C.) I'll be at the door for you at seven. We must be at barracks by the quarter. (GEORGE *crosses back,* L.) Poor devil! This comes of a man marrying beneath him.

Exit, HAWTREE, *door,* R. F.; GEORGE *comes down* L. *of table.*

Mar. I'm not sorry that he's gone, for I wanted to talk to you alone. Strange that a woman of such good birth as the Countess should encourage the attentions of Captain Hawtree for her daughter Florence. Lady Clardonax was one of the old Carburrys of Hampshire—not the Norfolk Carburrys but the direct line, and Mr. Hawtree's grandfather was in trade—something in the City—soap, I think, perhaps' pickles. (*points to stool; GEORGE brings it to her; she motions that he is to sit at her feet; GEORGE does so*) He's a very nice person, but parvenu as any one may see by his languor and his swagger. My boy (*kissing his forehead*), I am sure, will never make a mésalliance. He is a D'Alroy and by his mother's side, Planta Genista. The source of our life stream is Royal!

Geo. How is the Marquis?

Mar. Paralyzed. I left him at Spa with three physicians. He always is paralyzed at this time of the year; it's in the family. The paralysis is not personal but hereditary. I came over to see my steward; got to town last night.

Geo. How did you find me out here?

Mar. I sent the footman to the barracks, and he saw your man Dixon in the street, and Dixon gave him this address. It's so long since I've seen you. (*leans back in chair*) You're looking very well, and I daresay when mounted are quite a beau cavalier; and so, my boy (*playing with his hair*), you are going abroad for the first time on active service.

Geo. (*aside*) Every word can be heard in the next room—if they have only gone upstairs!

Mar. And now, my dear boy, before you go I want to give you some advice, and you mustn't despise it because I'm an old woman. We old women know a great deal more than people give us credit for. You are a soldier, so was your father, so was his father, so was mine, so was our Royal founder. We were born to lead—the common people expect it from us. It is our duty. Do you not remember in the chronicles of Froissart—(*with great enjoyment*)—I think I can quote it word for word. I've a wonderful memory for my age. (*with closed eyes*) It was in the 59th chapter how Godefroy D'Alroy helde the towne of St. Amande during the seige before Tournay. It said the towne was not closed but with pales, and Capt. argue there was Sir Amery of Pany, the Seneschall of Carcassonne, who had said it was not able to holde agaynst an hoeste, when one Godefroy D'Alroy say'd that rather then he woulde depart, he woulde keep it to the best of his power. Whereat the soldiers cheered and say'd "Lead us on, Sir Godefroy," and then began a fierce assault, and they within were chased, and sought for fro' streete to streete, but Godefroy stayed at the gate so valyantly, that the soldiers helde the towne until the comuynge of the Earl of Haynault with twelve thousand men.

Geo. I wish she'd go. If she once gets on to Froissart she'll never know when to stop. (*aside*)

Mar. When my boy fights, and you will fight over there, he is sure to distinguish himself; it his nature to. (*toys with his hair*) He cannot forget his birth, and when you meet these Asiatic ruffians who have dared to revolt and to outrage humanity, you will strike as your ancestor Galtier of Chevrault struck at Poictiers. Froissart mentions it thus: " Sir Galtier with his four squires was in the front of that battell, and there did marvels in arms, and Sir Galtier rode up to the Prince and said to him, ' Sir, take your horse and ride forth, this journey is yours; God is this day in your hands. Gette us to the French Kynge Catayle. I think verily by his valyantesse he woll not fly. Advance banner in the name of God and of Saynt George,' and Galtier gallopped forward to see his Kynges victory and meet his own death."

Geo. If Esther hears all this! (*aside*)

Mar. There is another subject about which I should have spoken to you before this, but an absurd prudery forbade me. I may never see you more. I am old, and you are going into battle (*kissing his forehead with emotion*) and this may be our last meeting. (*noise heard within folding doors*) What's that?

Geo. Nothing. My man—Dixon—in there.

Mar. We may not meet again on this earth. I do not fear your conduct my George, with men, but I know the temptations that beset a youth who is well born ; but a true soldier, a true gentleman, should not only be without fear but without reproach. It is easier to fight a famous man than to forego the conquest of a lovesick girl. A thousand Sepoys slain in battle cannot redeem the honor of a man who has betrayed the confidence of a confiding woman. Think, George, what a dishonor, what a stain upon your manhood, to hurl a girl to shame and degradation, and what excuse for it? That she is plebeian! A man of real honor will spare the woman who has confessed her love for him, as he would give quarter to an enemy he had disarmed. (*taking his hand*) Let my boy avoid the snares so artfully spread, and when he asks his mother to welcome the woman he has chosen for his wife, let me take her to my arms and plant a motherly kiss upon the white brow of a lady. (*noise of a fall heard within folding doors*)

Mar. (*rising*) What's that ?

Geo. Nothing ! (*rising*)

Mar. I heard a cry. (*goes up stage and throws open folding doors, discovering* ESTHER *lying on floor, with* POLLY *kneeling over her*)

Pol. George ! George !

GEORGE *goes up and raises* ESTHER *in his arms ;* POLLY *goes down,* L. *and wheels easy chair up* L. *for her ;* GEORGE *places* ESTHER *in chair,* GEORGE *on her* R., POLLY *on her* L.

Mar. (*coming down*, R.) Who are these *women?*

Pol. Women!

Mar. George D'Alroy, these persons should have been sent away. How could you dare to risk your mother meeting women of their stamp?

Pol. (*back*, L. C., *violently*) What does she mean? How dare she call us women? What's she I'd like to know?

Geo. Silence, Polly. You mustn't insult my mother.

Mar. The insult is from you. I leave you, and I hope that time may induce me to forget this scene of degradation. (*going up*, R.)

Geo. Stay mother. (MARQUISE *goes down a little*, R.) Before you go let me present to you Mrs. George D'Alroy, my wife. (GEORGE *has raised* ESTHER *from chair in both arms and supports her to up* C.)

Mar. Married!

Geo. Married. (*the* MARQUISE *sinks into easy chair*, R. GEORGE *replaces* ESTHER *in easy chair up* L., *but still retains her hand—two hesitating taps heard at door—*ECCLES *enters sneakingly*)

Ecc. They told us to come upstairs. When your man came, Polly was out, so I thought I should do instead. (*calling at door*) Come up, Sam. (enter SAM *in his Sunday clothes and smoking a cheroot*; *he nods and grins*)

Ecc. Sam had just called, so we three, Sam and I, and your man, all came in a hansom cab together. Didn't we, Sam?

ECCLES *and* SAM *go over to the girls*, L.

Mar. (*with glasses up, to* GEORGE) Who is this?

Geo. (*coming down* L. *of* MARQUISE) My wife's father.

ECCLES *comes down smilingly*, L.

Mar. What is he?

Geo. A—nothing.

Ecc. I am one of Nature's noblemen. Happy to see you, my lady. (*crosses to her*) Now my daughter told me who you are. (GEORGE *turns his back in an agony*) We old folks, father and mother of the young couple, ought to make friends. (*holding out his dirty hand*)

Mar. (*shrinking back*) Go away. What's his name?

ECCLES *goes up again disgusted*, L.

Geo. Eccles.

Mar. Eccles! Eccles! There never was an Eccles. He don't exist.

Ecc. (*coming down,* L.) Don't he? What d'ye call this? (*goes up again,* L., *and speaks to* SAM)

Mar. No Eccles was ever born.

Geo. He takes the liberty of breathing, notwithstanding. (*aside*) And I wish he wouldn't.

Mar. And who is the *little man?* Is he also Eccles?

SAM *looks round;* POLLY *gets close up to him, and looks with defiant glance at the* MARQUISE.

Geo. No.

Mar. Thank goodness! What, then?

Geo. His name is Gerridge.

Mar. Gerridge! It breaks one's teeth. Why is he here?

Geo. He is making love to Polly, my wife's sister.

Mar. And what is he?

Geo. A gasman.

Mar. He looks it! (GEORGE *goes up to* ESTHER, L.) And what is the—the sister?

ECCLES, *who has been casting longing eyes at the decanter on table, edges towards it and when he thinks no one is noticing, fills wine glass.*

Pol. (*asserting herself indignantly*) I'm in the ballet at the Theatre Royal, Lambeth—so was Esther. We're not ashamed of what we are. We have no cause to be.

Sam. (*back,* L. C.) That's right, Polly, pitch into the swells. Who are they? (*goes up a little*)

ECCLES *by this time has seized wine glass and turning his back is about to drink, when* HAWTREE *enters door,* R. *flat;* ECCLES *hides glass under his coat, and pretends to be looking up at picture*)

Haw. (*entering*) George! (*stops suddenly, looking round*) So all's known.

Mar. (*rising*) Captain Hawtree, see me to my carriage. I am broken-hearted. (*takes* HAWTREE'S *arm, crosses, is going up*)

Ecc. (*who simultaneously has tasted the claret spits it out again with a grimace exclaiming* "Rot." ESTHER *rises from chair in nervous excitement, clutching* GEORGE'S *hand*)

Geo. (*to* MARQUISE) Don't go in anger. You may not see me again. (MARQUISE *stops,* R. ; ESTHER *brings* GEORGE *down,* C.)

Est. (L. C., *with arm round his neck*) Oh! George, must you go?

Geo. Yes.

Est. I can't leave you—I'll go with you.

Geo. Impossible, the country is too unsettled.

Est. May I come after you?

Geo. Yes.

Est. (*with her head on his shoulder*) I may!

Mar. (*coming down, R.*) It is his duty to go—his honor calls him. The honor of his family—*our* honor!

Est. But I love him so. Pray don't be angry with me.

Haw. (*looking at watch and coming down, C.*) George!

Geo. I must go, love. (HAWTREE *goes up, R. C.*)

Mar. (*advancing*) Let me arm you, George—let your mother, as in the days of old. There is blood and blood, my son, let Radicals and rebels rave as they will—see, your wife cries, when she should be proud of you.

Geo. My Esther is all that is true, good, and noble. No lady born to a coronet could be gentler or more true. Esther, my wife, fetch me my sword, and buckle my belt round me. (*whispers to* ESTHER) It will please my mother. (*to* MARQUISE) You shall see. (ESTHER *totters up stage, L., and brings down his sword,* POLLY *his cap; as* ESTHER *is trying to buckle his belt he whispers*) I've left money for you, my darling. My lawyer will call on you to-morrow. Forgive me, I tried to tell you we were ordered for India, but when the time came my heart failed me and I——

ESTHER, *before she can succeed in fastening his sword belt, reels and falls fainting in his arms—*POLLY *hurries to her, L., and takes her hand—*SAM *standing at piano looking frightened—*ECCLES *at back very little concerned—*HAWTREE *with hand upon handle of door, R. F., and* MARQUISE *looking on R. of* GEORGE.

ACT DROP.

For Call.—ESTHER *in chair fainting—*POLLY *and* SAM *each side of her holding her hands—the folding doors, L. C., thrown open and* ECCLES *standing within holding up bottle of brandy to the light, with triumphant grin on his face.*

ACT III.

Scene.—*The room in Stangate (as in Act I.)—*POLLY *discovered, dressed in black, seated at table, R. corner of it—she is placing the skirt in bandbox as curtain rises.*

Pol. (*placing skirt in box and leaning her chin upon her hand.*) There, there's the dress for poor Esther in case she gets the engagement, which I don't suppose she will; it's too good luck, and good luck never comes to her, poor thing. (*rises and goes up to cradle,* *up* c.) Baby's asleep still. How good he looks, as good as if he were dead, like his poor father, and alive too at the same time, like his dear self. Oh dear me, it's a strange world. (*sits again as before, feeling in pocket for money*) Four and elevenpence ; that must do for to-day and to-morrow. Esther's going to bring in the rusks for Georgie. (*takes up slate*) Three, 5, 8 and 4, 12, 1 shilling. Um, father can only have twopence ; he must make do with that till Saturday, when I get my salary. If Esther gets the engagement I shan't have many more salaries to take. I shall leave the stage and retire into private life. I wonder if I shall like private life, and if private life will like me. It will seem so strange being no longer Miss Mary Eccles—Mary Eccles—but Mrs. Samuel Gerridge. (*writes it on slate*) Mrs. Samuel Garridge. (*laughs bashfully*) La ! To think of my being Mrs. Anybody. How annoyed Susan Smith will be. (*writing on slate*) Mrs. Samuel Gerridge presents her compliments to Miss Susan Smith, and Mrs. Samuel Gerridge requests the favor of Miss Susan Smith's company to tea on Tuesday evening next, at Mrs. Samuel Gerridge's house. (*pause*) Poor Susan ! (*beginning again*) P. S., Mrs. Samuel Gerridge——(*knock heard at room door ;* POLLY *starts*)

Sam. (*without*) Polly, open the door.

Pol. Sam ! (*wipes out note on slate*) Come in.

Sam. (*without*) I can't.

Pol. Why not ?

Sam. I've got something on my head.

POLLY *rises and opens door,* R.—SAM *enters, carrying a small table on his head ; he has a rule pocket in corduroys ; rule seen.*

Pol. What's that ? (*shuts door*)

Sam. Furniture. (*going down,* R. *and depositing table*) How are you, my Polly ? (*kissing her*) Bless you, you look handsomer than ever this morning. (*dances and sings*) Fiddle-de tum-ti-di-do.

Pol. What's the matter, Sam, are you mad ?

Sam. No, happy ; much the same thing.

Pol. Where have you been these two days ?

Sam. That's just what I'm going to tell you. Polly, my pet, my brightest batswing and most brilliant burner, what do you think ?

Pol. Oh, do go on, Sam, or I'll slap your face.

Sam. Well, you've heard me speak of old Binks the plumber, and glazier, and gasfitter, who died six months ago ?

Pol. Yes.

Sam. I've bought his business. (*sits on table*)

Pol. No !

Sam. Yes, of his widow, Mrs. Binks. So much down, so much more at the end of the year. (*dances and sings up,* R.) Ri ti toodle, roodle oodle. Ri ti tooral ororal lay.

Pol. (*sitting on chair,* L. *end of table*) La, Sam!

Sam. (*pacing stage up and down*) Yes, I've bought the good-will, fixtures, fittings, stock, rolls of gas pipe, and sheets of lead. (*sits on table facing* POLLY) I am a tradesman with a shop, a master tradesman; all I want to complete the premises is a missus. (*tries to kiss her; she slaps his face*)

Pol. Sam, don't be foolish! (*she goes up* L. *of table, taking the slate up with her*)

Sam. (*following*) Come and be Mrs. Sam Gerridge, Polly, my patent safety day and night light. You'll furnish me completely. (POLLY *puts slate on table up* L., SAM *snatches it up and looks at it; she snatches it from him with a shriek and rubs out writing, looking daggers at him—he comes down stage,* L., *with a grin*)

Pol. Only to think!

Sam. (*coming down with* POLLY) I spent all yesterday looking up furniture. I bought that a bargain. (*opens drawer of table,* R.) And I brought it to show you for your approval. I've bought lots of other things, and I'll bring 'em all here to show you for your approval.

Pol. I couldn't think what had become of you.

Sam. Look here. (*producing patterns of paper*) I want you to choose the pattern for the back parlor behind the shop. I'll new paper it and new paint it, and new furnish it. It shall be all bran new.

Pol. (L. *of table*) But won't it cost a lot of money, Sam?

Sam. I can work for it. With customers in the shop, and you in the back parlor, I can work like fifty men. (*sits on table,* R. C., *with arm round* POLLY) Only fancy at night when the shop's closed and the shutters are up, counting out the till together. Besides, that isn't all I've done; I've been writing, and what I've written I've got printed.

Pol. No!

Sam. True.

Pol. You've been writing about me. (*delighted*)

Sam. No, about the shop. (POLLY *disgusted*) Here it is. (*takes roll of circulars from pocket*) You mustn't laugh; you know it's my first attempt. I wrote it the night before last, and when I thought of you, Polly, the words seemed to flow like red hot solder. (*reads*) "Sam Gerridge takes this opportunity of informing the nobility, gentry, and inhabitants of the Borough Road." You know there's not many of the nobility and gentry live in the Borough Road; but it pleases the inhabitants to make 'em believe you think so, "Of informing the nobility, gentry, and inhabitants of the Borough Road, and its vicinity"—that's rather good, I think? (*looking at her*)

Pol. Yes; I've heard worse.

Sam. I first thought of saying neighborhood, but I thought vicinity sounded more genteel. " And its vicinity, that he has entered upon the business of the late Mr. Binks, his relict, the present Mrs. B., having disposed to him of the same." Now listen, Polly, because it gets interesting—" S. G.—"

Pol. S. G. Who's he?

Sam. Me, S. G., Samuel Gerridge, me—us—we're S. G. Don't interrupt me or you'll cool my metal and then I can't work. " S. G., hopes by a constant attention to business and "—mark this—" by supplying the best articles at the most reasonable prices, to merit a continuance of those favors which it will ever be his constant study to deserve." There ! (*turning on table to* R., *triumphantly*) Stop a bit—there's more yet—" bell-hanging, gas-fitting, plumbing and glazing as usual." There—it's all my own. (*puts circular on mantelpiece, crosses,* R., *contemplates it*) And now, Polly (*taking his table up,* R.; *postman's knock*) I'll go—I shall send some of these out by post. (*goes off* R. D., *and returns with letter*)

Pol. (*taking it*) Oh ! for Esther. I know who it's from. (*places letter on mantelpiece, seriously*) Sam, who do you think was here last night ?

Sam. Who?

Pol. Captain Hawtree. (*comes across,* L. C.)

Sam. (*depreciatingly*) Oh, come back from India, I suppose ?

Pol. Yes ; luckily Esther was out.

Sam. I never liked that long swell. He was an uppish, conceited——

Pol. (*sitting* L. *end of table*) Oh, he's better than he used to be. He's a major now. He's only been in England a fortnight.

Sam. (L.) Did he tell you anything about poor D'Alroy ?

Pol. (*leaning against table end*) Yes ; he said he was riding out not far from the cantonment, and was surrounded by a troop of Sepoy cavalry, which took him prisoner and galloped off with him.

Sam. But about his death ?

Pol. Oh ! (*hiding her face*) Oh ! that, he said, was believed to be too terrible to mention.

Sam. Did he tell you anything else ?

Pol. No ; he asked a lot of questions, and I told him everything. How poor Esther had taken her widowhood, and what a dear good baby the baby was, and what a comfort to us all, and how Esther had come back to live with us again.

Sam. And the reason for it ? (*sharply*)

Pol. (*looking down*) Yes.

Sam. How your father got the money that was left for Esther ?

Pol. Don't say any more about that, Sam. (*sharply*)

Sam. I only think Captain Hawtree ought to know where the money did go, and that you shouldn't screen your father and let him suppose that you and Esther spent it all.

Pol. I told him.

Sam. Did you tell him that your father was always at harmonic meetings, at taverns, and had half-cracked himself by drink, and was always singing the songs and making the speeches that he heard there, and that he was always going on about his wrongs as one of the working classes? He's a pretty one for one of the working classes—he is! Hasn't done a stroke of work these twenty years. Now, I am one of the working classes, but I don't howl about it. I only work and I don't spout. (*goes up* C., *and comes down again*)

Pol. Hold your tongue, Sam. I won't have you say any more against poor father. He has his faults, but he's a very clever man. (*sighing*)

Sam. Oh! What else did Captain Hawtree say?

Pol. He advised us to apply to Mr. D'Alroy's mother.

Sam. The Marquissy? And what did you say?

Pol. I said that Esther wouldn't hear of it, and so the Major said that he'd write to Esther, and I suppose this is the letter.

Sam. Now, Polly, come and choose the paper. (*going up*, C.)

Pol. (*rising*) Can't; who's to mind baby?

Sam. (*at window*) There's your father passing, won't he mind him?

Pol. (*going up*, C.) I daresay he will. If I promise him an extra sixpence on Saturday. (*tapping at window*) Hi! Father!

Sam. (*aside*) He looks down in the mouth. I suppose he's had no drink. (*goes down*, R.)

Enter ECCLES *in shabby black ; taking half circle of stage, he sits before fire,* L.

Ecc. No, not for long. (*placing hat on table*) Good morning, Samuel. Going back to work—that's right, my boy. Stick to it! (*pokes fire*) Stick to it! Nothing like it!

Sam. (*down*, R. C.; *aside*) Now isn't that too bad. No, Mr. Eccles, I've knocked off for the day. (*crosses to him*)

Ecc. (*waving poker*) That's bad—that's bad. Nothing like work for the young. I don't work so much as I used to myself; but I like to see the young uns at it. It does me good, and it does them good too. What does the poet say? (*rising impressively*)

> " A carpenter said, tho' that was well spoke,
> It was better by far to defend it with oak ;
> A currier, wiser than both these together,
> Said, say what you will there is nothing like labor.
> For a' that, an' a' that,
> Your ribbon, gown, and a' that ;
> The rank is but the guinea stamp,
> The working man's the gold for a' that.''

(*sits again, triumphantly wagging his head*)

Sam. (*aside*) This is the sort of public-house loafer that wants the wages and no work, an idle old——(*goes up in disgust*)

Pol. (*on* ECCLES' L.) Esther will be in by and bye. Do, father. (ECCLES: *No, no, I tell you I won't*) (*whispering; arm around his neck*) And I'll give you sixpence extra on Saturday.

Ecc. Oh! Very well. (POLLY *gets hat and cloak from peg up* R.) Oh, you puss, you know how to get over your poor old father.

Sam. (*aside*) Yes ; with sixpence.

Pol. (*putting on bonnet and cloak*) Give the cradle a rock if baby cries, father.

Sam. If you should want employment or amusement, Mr. Eccles, cast your eye over that. (*gives him circular and* exit *with* POLLY, D. R.; ECCLES *lights pipe and stands with back to fire, smoking vigorously ; a pause*)

Ecc. Poor Esther! nice market she's brought her pigs to. Ugh! Mind the baby indeed ; what good is he to me? That fool of a girl to throw away all her chances—*a honorabless*—and her father not to have a quartern of cool refreshing gin ; stopping in here to rock a young honorable ; cuss him! (L. *of cradle, rocking it*) Are we slaves, we working men? (*sings savagely*) Britons never, never, never shall be—(*dashes pipe into fireplace, and going down, sits at end of table,* L. *of it ; nodding his head sagaciously ; hands in his trousers pockets*) However, I won't stand this much longer ; I've writ to the old cat, I mean to the Marquissy, to tell her that her daughter-in-law and her grandson is almost starving. That fool Esther, too proud to write to her for money. I hate pride, it's beastly! (*rising*) There's no beastly pride about me. (*goes up* R. *of table, smacking his lips*) I'm as dry as a lime kiln. (*crosses to mantelpiece and takes up dram bottle*) Empty. (*replaces it, takes up jug from table*) Milk. (*with disgust*) For this young aristocratic pauper ; everybody in the house is sacrificed for him. (*at foot of cradle,* R. C., *with hands on chair back*) And to think that a working man, and a member of the Committee of the Banded Brothers for the regeneration of human kind by means of equal diffusion of intelligence and equal division of property should be thirsty while this cub—(*draws apart curtain and looks at child—after a pause*) That there coral he's got round his neck is *gold*, real *gold* (*with hand on knot at end of cradle,* R. C.,) Oh! society! Oh! Governments! Oh! Class Legislature—*is this right?* Shall this mindless wretch enjoy himself while sleeping with a jewelled gaud, and his poor old grandfather wants the price of half-pint? *No*, it shall not be. Rather than see it I will myself resent this outrage on the rights of man, and in this holy crusade of class against class, of weak and lowly against the powerful and the strong, (*pointing to child*) I will strike one blow for freedom. (*goes to back of cradle*) He's asleep. It will fetch ten bob round the corner, and if the

Marquissy gives us anything it can be got out with some o' that. (*steals coral*) Lie still, my darllng. It's grandfather's a-watching you!

> " Who ran to catch me when I fell,
> And kicked the place to make it well——
> My grandfather."

As he is going off at door, R., **enter** ESTHER ; *she is dressed like a widow, pale face, and her manner quick, stern, and imperious ; she carries a parcel and paper bag of rusks in her hand.*

Ecc. My love !

ESTHER *passes, puts parcel on table, goes to cradle, kneels down and kisses child*—ECCLES *fumbles with the lock nervously, and is going out as* ESTHER *speaks*)

Est. My Georgie ! Where's his coral? Gone ! Father,—(*rising* ; ECCLES *stops*)—the coral ! Where is it?

Ecc. (*confused*) Where's what ?

Est. The coral ! You've got it ; I know it. Give it me. (*quickly and imperiously*) Give it me—*give it me.* (ECCLES *takes coral from his pocket and gives it back*)

Est. If you *dare* to touch *my* child ! (*goes to cradle*)

Ecc. Esther, am I not your father ? (*coming down*, R. ESTHER *gets round table to* L. C.)

Est. And I am his mother.

Ecc. (*coming down*) Do you bandy words with me, you pauper, to whom I have given shelter, shelter to you and your brat. I've a good mind—(*advancing to her with clenched fist*)

Est. (*confronting him*) If you dare ! I am no longer your little drudge, your frightened servant. When mother died and I was so high, I tended you, and worked for you, and you beat me. That time is past. I am a woman, I am a wife, a widow, a mother. Do you think I will let you outrage *him ?* (*pointing to cradle*) Touch me if you dare ! (*advancing a step*)

Ecc. (*bursting into tears*) And ·this is my own child which I nursed when a baby, and sung cuotsicum coo to afore she could speak. Honorable Mrs, D'Alroy, I forgive you for all that you have said. In everything that I have done I've acted with the best intentions. May the babe in that cradle never treat you as you have tret me—a grey 'air'd father. May he never cease to love and *h*onor you as you have ceased to love and *h*onor me, after all that I've done for you, and the position to which I've raised you by my own industry. May he never behave to you like the bad daughters of King Lear; and may you never live to feel how sharper than a serpent's scales it is to have a thankless child.

Exit, R. D.

Est. (*kneeling by cradle*) My darling! (*arranging bed and placing coral to the baby's lips and then to her own*) Mamma's come back to her own. Did she stay away from him so long? (*rises and looks at the sabre, etc.*) My George, to think you never can look upon his face, nor hear his voice! My brave gallant, and handsome husband! My lion and my love! (*comes down,* C., *pacing the stage*) Oh! to be a soldier, and to fight the wretches who destroyed him, who took my darling from me! (*action of cutting with sabre*) To gallop miles upon their upturned faces! (*crosses* L. *with action ; sees letter*) What's this! Captain Hawtree's hand. (*reads*) "My dear Mrs. D'Alroy, I returned to England less than a fortnight ago. I have some papers and effects of my poor friend's, which I am anxious to deliver to you, and I beg of you to name a day when I can call with them and see you. At the same time let me express my deepest sympathy with your affliction. Your husband's loss was mourned by every man in the regiment. (ESTHER *lays the letter on her heart and then resumes reading*) I have heard with great pain of the pecuniary embarrassments into which accident and the imprudence of others have placed you. I trust you will not consider me, one of poor George's oldest comrades and friends, either intrusive or impertinent in sending the enclosed—(*she takes out cheque*)—and in hoping that should any further difficulties arise you will inform me of them, and remember that I am, dear Mrs. D'Alroy, now and always, your faithful and sincere friend, ARTHUR HAWTREE." (ESTHER *goes to cradle and bends over it*) Oh, his boy, if you could read it! (*crosses*)

Enter, POLLY, R. D.

Pol. Father gone?

Est. Polly, you look quite flurried. (POLLY *laughs and whispers to* ESTHER)

Est. (*near head of table taking* POLLY *in her arms and kissing her*) So soon! well, my darling, I hope you may be happy. (*sobs*)

Pol. (*crosses* L. *round table and putting rusks in saucepan*) Did you see the agent, dear?

Est. (R. *of table*) Yes ; the manager didn't come, he broke his appointment again.

Pol. (L. *of table*) Nasty rude fellow!

Est. (*seated*) The agent said it didn't matter. He thought I should get the engagement; he'll only give me thirty shillings a week though.

Pol. But you said that two pounds was the regular salary.

Est. (*handkerchief to eyes*) Yes, but they know I'm poor, and want the engagement, and so take advantage of me. (*with her handkerchief to her eyes*)

Pol. I put the dress in the bandbox ; it looks almost as good as new.

Est. (*seated*) I've had a letter from Captain Hawtree.

Pol. I know, dear, he came here last night.

Est. A dear good letter, speaking of George, and enclosing me a cheque for £30.

Pol. (*up at cupboard*) Oh, how kind! You mustn't let father know of it. (*coming down to table—noise of carriage wheels without*)

Est. I shan't.

ECCLES enters, *breathless ;* ESTHER *rises ;* POLLY *runs to window.*

Ecc. It's the Marquissy in her coach. Now be civil to her, and she may do something for us ; I see the coach as I was coming from the Rainbow. (POLLY *places chairs in order*)

Ecc. (*at door*) This way, my lady ; up them steps ; they're rather awkward for anybody like you, but them as is poor and lowly must do as best they can with steps and circumstances.

ESTHER *and* POLLY, L. *at end of table*—enter MARQUISE, D. R. ; *she surveys the place with aggressive astonishment*—ESTHER *drops the costume into bandbox, and* POLLY *puts the lid on it.*

Mar. (*half aside, going down,* R.) What a hole, and for my grandson to breathe such an atmosphere, and to be contaminated by such associations. (*to* ECCLES, *who is a little up,* R. C.) Which is the young woman who married my son?

Est. I am Mrs. D'Alroy, widow of George D'Alroy. Who are you?

Mar. I am his mother, the Marquise de St. Maur.

Est. (*with a grand air*) Be seated, I beg.

Mar. (*rejecting chair offered servilely by* ECCLES, *and looking round*) The chairs are all dirty. (SAM enters *with an easy chair on his head, which he puts down,* L. *not seeing* MARQUISE, *who instantly sits down in it, concealing it completely*)

Sam. (*astonished,* L. *corner*) It's the Marquissy. (*looking at her*) These here aristocrats are fine women though. Plenty of 'em. (*describing circle*) Quality and quantity.

Pol. (L. *of table end*) Sam, you'd better come back. (ECCLES *nudges him and bustles him towards door*)

Sam. (*going towards door, aside*) She's here. What's coming, I wonder ! (*exit* SAM ; ECCLES *shuts door on him*)

Ecc. (*coming down,* R. C., *rubbing his hands*) If we'd a-know'd your ladyship had bin a-coming we'd a had the place cleaned up a bit. (*with hands on chair back ;* ESTHER *snatches chair from him ; he gets round to* R., *behind* MARQUISE)

Mar. (*to* ESTHER) You remember me, do you not?

Est. Perfectly, though I only saw you once. (*seating herself on* *grande dame,* L. C.) May I ask what has procured me the honor of this visit?

Mar. I was informed that you were in want and I came here to offer you assistance.

Est. I thank you for your offer, and the delicate consideration for my feelings with which it is made. I need no assistance.

Mar. A letter I received last night informed me that you did.

Est. May I ask if that letter came from Captain Hawtree?

Mar. No, from this person, your father, I think.

Est. (*to* ECCLES) How dare you interfere in my affairs?

Ecc. My love, I did it with the best intentions.

Mar. Then you will not accept assistance from me?

Est. No.

Pol. (*aside to* ESTHER, *holding her hand*) Bless you, my darling.

Mar. But you have a child—a son—my grandson. (*with emotion*)

Est. Master D'Alroy wants for nothing.

Pol. (*aside*) And never shall!

Mar. I came here to propose that my grandson should go back with me.

Est. (*rising defiantly*) What, part with my boy? I'd sooner die!

Mar. You can see him when you wish—as for money I——

Est. Not for ten thousand million worlds—not for ten thousand million marchionesses.

Ecc. Better do what the good lady asks you, my dear. She's advising you for your good and for the child's likewise.

Mar. Surely you cannot intend to bring up my son's son in a place like this? (ESTHER *goes up,* C.)

Ecc. It is a poor place, and we are poor people, sure enough. We ought not to fly in the faces of our pastors and masters—our pastresses and mistresses.

Pol. Oh, hold your tongue, do. (*aside; goes up to cradle*)

Est. (*before cradle*) Master George D'Alroy will remain with his mother. The offer to take him from her is an insult to his dead father and to him.

Ecc. He don't seem to feel it, stuck up little beast.

Mar. But you have no money. How can you rear him? How can you educate him? How can you live?

Est. (*tearing dress from bandbox*) Turn Columbine! Go on the stage again and dance.

Mar. (*rising*) You are insolent. You forget that I am a lady.

Est. You forget that I am a mother. (*replaces dress in box*) Do you dare to offer to buy my child, his breathing image, his living memory, with money? (*crosses to door,* R., *and throws it open*) There is the door. Go! (*picture*)

Ecc. (*to* MARQUISE, *who has risen*) Very sorry, my lady, as you should be tret in this way, which was not my wishes.

Mar. Silence! (ECCLES *retreats,* R., *putting back chair;* MAR-QUISE *goes up to door,* R.) Mrs. D'Alroy, if anything could have increased my sorrow for the wretched marriage my poor son was decoyed into, it would be your conduct this day to his mother. (exit, R. D.)

Ecc. (*looking after her at door,* R.) To go away and not leave a sou behind her. Cat! cat! stingy cat! (*crosses to fire* L., *sits and pokes it violently—carriage wheels heard without—*POLLY *goes and kisses* ESTHER *up* C.)

Est. Take me to my room. I'll lie down. Let me have the baby or that old woman may come back and steal him.

Exeunt, ESTHER *and* POLLY *with the baby,* R. D.

Ecc. (*rocking in chair*) Well, women is the obstinatest devils that never wore horse shoes. (*striking table*) Children! beasts! beasts!

Enter, SAM *and* POLLY, R. D.

Sam. I'll tell him now and get it over at once. (POLLY *takes bandbox from table and places it up* L. *corner*) And now, Mr. Eccles, since you've been talking on family affairs, I'd like to have a word with you, so take this opportunity to——

Ecc. (*raising his head sharply*) Take what you like and then order more. (*rising and down,* L. C.) Samuel Gerridge, that hand is a hand that never turned its back on a friend or a bottle to give him. (*sings*) I will stand by my friend, if he'll stand to me, me, gentlemen.

Sam. Well, Mr. Eccles, sir, it's this.

Pol. (*aside; coming down* R. *of table*) Don't tell him too sudden, Sam, it might shock his feelings. (*goes round and sits* L. *of table end*)

Sam. It's this. You know that for the past four years I've been keeping company with Mary—Polly. (POLLY *sits* L., *behind end of table*)

Ecc. (*sinking into chair*) Go it, go it. Strike home, young man, strike on this grey head. (*sings*) Britons, strike home, home here! (*tapping his chest*) To my heart, don't spare me. Have a go at my grey hairs. Pull 'em, pull 'em out, a long pull, a strong pull, and a pull altogether. (*cries and drops his face on arm upon table*)

Pol. (L. *of table*) Oh, father, I wouldn't hurt your feelings for the world. (*kissing him*)

Sam. (*crosses to* ECCLES) Mr. Eccles, I wouldn't wish to annoy you, sir, but now I'm going to enter upon a business. Here's a circular. (*giving one*)

Ecc. (*indignantly*) What are circulars compared to a father's feelings?

Sam. And I wish Polly to name the day, sir, and so I ask you.

Ecc. This is 'ard. This is 'ard. *This is 'ard.* One o' my gals marries a so-dger, the other goes a gasfitting.

Sam. The business, which will enable me to maintain a wife, is that of the late Mr. Binks, plumber, glazier, etc.

Ecc. (*sings*) They have given thee to a plumber! They have broken every vow. They have given thee to a plumber, and my heart is breaking now, now, gentlemen.

Pol. You know, father, you can come and see me.

Ecc. (*rising and holding out his hand*) So I can and that's a comfort, (*shaking her hand*) and you can see me, and that's a comfort ; I'll come and see you often—every day (SAM *turns up stage in horror*) and crack a fatherly bottle, and shed a friendly tear.

Pol. Do, father, do.

Sam. (*with a gulp*) Yes, Mr. Eccles, do.

Ecc. I will. (*he takes the hand of each and goes down with them*) And this it is to be a father. (*puts hat on from bureau and returns,* C.) I would part with any of my children for their own good readily if I was paid for it. (*sings*) For I know that the angels are whispering to me—me, gentlemen.

Sam. I will make Polly a good husband, and anything that I can do to prove it (*lowering his voice*) in the way of spirituous liquors and tobacco (*slipping coin into his hand unseen by* POLLY) shall be done.

Ecc. (*lighting up*) " Be kind to thy father, wherever you be, for he is a blessing and credit to thee—thee, gentlemen." (*goes up,* R.) Well, my children, bless you ; take the blessing of a grey-hair'd father. (POLLY *sobbing ;* ECCLES *comes down,* C., *to* SAM) Samuel Gerridge, she shall be thine. You shall be her husband. (*looking at money*) A friend is awaiting for me outside which I want to have a word with, and may you never know how much more sharper than a serpent's tooth it is to have a marriageable daughter. (*sings*)

> " When I heard he was married,
>   I breathed not a tone,
>   The h'eyes of all round me
>   Was fixed on my own.
>   I flew to my chamber
>   To hide my despair ;
>   I tore the bright circlet
>   Of gems from my hair.
>   When I heard she was married.
>   When I heard she was——   Exit, *door*, R.

(*without*) Married, gentlemen.''

Pol. (*drying her eyes*) There, Sam, I always told you that though father had his faults his heart was in the right place.

Sam. (*at end of table, aside*) Poor Polly! (*goes up, a knock at* R. *door;* SAM *sits on table,* L.)

Pol. Come in!

Enter, HAWTREE *in black.*

Haw. I met the Marquise's carriage on the bridge. Has she been here? (SAM *crosses to fire and stands with back to it*)

Pol. Yes.

Haw. What happened?

Pol. Oh, she wanted to take away the child. (*crosses round to cupboard up* L.)

Sam. In the coach.

Haw. And what did Mrs. D'Alroy say to that?

Sam. Mrs. D'Alroy said she'd see her flow'd first, or words to that effect.

Haw. I am sorry to hear this. I had hoped—however, that's over.

Pol. Yes, it's over, and I hope we shall hear no more about it. Want to take away the child indeed! Like her impudence! What next! (*getting ready tea things*) Esther's gone to lie down. I shan't wake her up for tea, though she's had nothing to eat all day.

Sam. (L. *of table*) Shall I fetch some shrimps?

Pol. (L. *of table*) No ; what made you think of shrimps?

Sam. They're a relish, and consoling—at least I always find 'em so. (SAM *goes up and pulls down blind*)

Pol. I won't ask you, Major, to take tea with us, you're too grand.

Haw. (*placing hat on piano*) Not at all ; I shall be most happy. (*aside*) 'Pon my word, these are a very good sort of people. I'd no idea——(*sits* R. *of table,* POLLY *and* SAM, L.)

Pol. Sam, light the gas.

Sam. No, don't light up ; I like this sort of dusk. It's unbusinesslike but pleasant. (*puts his arm round her waist*)

Pol. (*making tea*) Sugar, Sam?

Sam. (*aside*) Look in the cup.

Pol. (*to* HAWTREE, *handing cup*) You want sweetening. Sugar yourself—we've got no milk. It'll be here directly—it's just his time.

Voice. (*outside and rattle of milk pails*) Milk-oow!

Pol. There he is. (*knock at door,* R.) Oh, I know, I owe him fourpence. (*feeling her pockets—knock again louder*)

Pol. He's very impatient. Come in.

Enter, GEORGE, *his face bronzed, and in full health; he carries a milk can in his hand, which he places on table.*

Geo. A fella hung this on the railings, so I brought it in.

POLLY *and* SAM *slip frightened under the table*—HAWTREE *remains motionless and terrified*—GEORGE *astonished*—*picture.*

Geo. What's the matter with you?
Haw. (*rising*) George!
Geo. Hawtree! you here?
Pol. O-o-o-o-oh! The ghost! The ghost!
Sam. It shan't hurt you, Polly. Perhaps it's only indigestion.
Haw. Then you're not dead?
Geo. Dead! no! Where's my wife?
Haw. You were reported killed.
Geo. It wasn't true!
Haw. Alive! my old friend, alive!
Geo. And well. (*shakes hands*) Landed this morning. Where's my wife?
Sam. (*who has popped his head from under tablecloth*) He isn't dead, Poll, he's alive! (*pause*)
Pol. Alive! My dear George! Oh, my dear brother! (*looking at him intently*) Alive! (*hysterically, going to him*) Oh, my dear, dear, dear brother! (*in his arms*) How could you go and do so?

SAM *down,* L. GEORGE *places* POLLY *in his arms.*

Geo. Where's Esther?
Haw. Here—in this house.
Geo. Here! Doesn't she know I'm back?
Pol. No! how should she?
Geo. (*to* HAWTREE) Didn't you get my telegram?
Haw. No. Where from?
Geo. Southampton. I sent it to the club.
Haw. I haven't been there these three days.
Pol. (*gushingly*) Oh, my dear, dear, dear, dead and gone, come back all alive brother George!

GEORGE *passes her down to* R. C.

Sam. (*crosses,* C.) Glad to see you, sir.
Geo. Thank you, Gerridge. (*shakes hands*) Same to you. But Esther!
Pol. (*back to audience and kerchief to her eyes*) She's asleep in her room. (GEORGE *is going,* R. D. POLLY *stops him*) You mustn't see her.
Geo. Not see her after this long absence! Why not?

Haw. She's so ill to-day ; she has been greatly excited. The news of your death, which we all mourned, has shaken her terribly.

Geo. Poor girl! poor girl!

Pol. (*down*, R. C.) Oh! we all cried so when you died, (*crying*) and now you're alive again I want to cry ever so much more. (*crying*)

Haw. We must break the news to her by degrees. (*crosses behind to fire*)

Sam. If we turn the tap on its full pressure she'll explode. (*goes up*)

Geo. To return and not to be able to see her, to love her, to kiss her! (*stamps*)

Pol. Hush!

Geo. I forgot, I should wake her!

Pol. More than that—you'll wake the baby.

Geo. Baby! What baby?

Pol. Yours.

Geo. Mine!

Pol. Yes, yours and Esther's. Why, didn't you know there was a baby? La, the ignorance of these men!

Haw. Yes, George, you're a father.

Geo. Why wasn't I told this? Why didn't you write?

Pol. How could we when you were dead?

Sam. And hadn't left your address.

Geo. If I can't see Esther I will see the child. The sight of me won't be too much for its nerves. Where is it?

Pol. Sleeping in its mother's arms. (GEORGE *goes to door*, R. *they stop him*) Please not! Please not!

Geo. I must! I will!

Pol. It might kill her, and you wouldn't like to do that. I'll fetch the baby, but oh, please don't make a noise.

                                        Exit, POLLY, R. D.

Geo. My baby, my ba——It's a dream. You've seen it. What's it like?

Sam. Oh, it's like a—like a sort of—infant, white and milky, and all that.

Enter, POLLY *with baby wrapped in shawl ;* GEORGE *meets* POLLY, C.

Pol. Gently, gently, take care. (*giving child to* GEORGE) Esther will hardly have it touched.

Geo. But I'm its father.

Pol. That don't matter. She's very particular.

Geo. Boy or girl?

Pol. Guess.

Geo. Boy? (POLLY *nods*—GEORGE *enraptured*) What's its name?

Pol. Guess.

Geo. George? (POLLY *nods*) Eustace? (POLLY *nods*) Fairfax? Algernon? (POLLY *nods—pause*) My names.

Sam. (*to* HAWTREE *as they go up*) There don't seem room enough in him, sir, to hold so many names, do there?

Geo. To come back all the way from India to find that I'm dead, and that you're alive! To find my wife a widow with a new love, aged—how old are you? I'll buy you a pony to-morrow, my brave little boy. What's his weight? I should say two pound nothing. You *are* a surprise, my—(*affected, touching him*) Take him away, Polly, for fear I should bend him. (POLLY *takes child and places it in cradle*)

Haw. (*crosses to* R. *corner;* SAM *takes his place*) But tell us how it is you're back, how you escaped.

Geo. (R. C., *coming down*) Too long a story just now, by-and-by. Tell *me* all about it. (POLLY *gives him chair,* R. C.) How is it Esther's living here?

Pol. (L. *of table; after a pause*) She came back here after the child was born, and the furniture was sold up.

Geo. Sold up! What furniture?

Pol. That you bought for her.

Haw. It couldn't be helped, George; Mrs. D'Alroy was so poor.

Geo. Poor! but I left her £600 to put in the bank.

Haw. We must tell you; she gave it to her father, who banked it in his own name.

Sam. And lost it in betting; every copper.

Geo. Then she's been in want?

Pol. No, not in want; friends lent her money.

Geo. (*seated,* R. C.) What friends? (*pause; to* HAWTREE) You?

Pol. Yes.

Geo. (*rising and shaking* HAWTREE'S *hand*) Thank you, old fella. (HAWTREE *goes up*)

Sam. (*aside*) Who'd ha thought that long swell had it in him! He never mentioned it.

Geo. So papa Eccles had the money?

Sam. And blued it.

Pol. (*pleadingly, both hands on end of table*) You see father was very unlucky on the race course. He told us that if it hadn't been that all his calculations were upset by a horse winning that had no business to, he should have made all our fortunes. Father's been unlucky, and he gets tipsy at times, but he's a very clever man, if you only give him scope enough.

Sam. I'd give him scope enough!

Geo. Where is he now?

Sam. Public-house.

Geo. And how is he?

Sam. Drunk!

Geo. (*rising, to* HAWTREE) You were right.   There is something in Caste. (*aloud*) But tell us about it. (*sits*)

Pol. Well, you know you went away, and then the baby was born. Oh! he was such a sweet little thing—just like—your eyes——

Geo. Cut that.

Pol. Well, baby came, and when baby was six days old your letter came, Major. (*to* HAWTREE) I saw it was from India, and that it wasn't in your hand (*to* GEORGE) I guessed what was inside it, so I opened it unknown to her, and I read there of your capture and death. I daren't tell her. I went to father to ask his advice, but he was too tipsy to understand me. Sam fetched the doctor. He told us that the news would kill her. When she woke up she said she had dreamt there was a letter from you. I told her no, and day after day she asked for a letter. So the doctor advised us to write one as if it came from you. So we did, Sam and I, and the doctor told her—told Esther, I mean—that her eyes were bad and she musn't read, and we read our letter to her, didn't we, Sam? But bless you, she always knew it hadn't come from you. At last when she was stronger we told her all.

Geo. (*after a pause*) How did she take it?

Pol. She pressed the baby in her arms and turned her face to the wall. (*a pause,* GEORGE *sits*) Well, to make a long story short, when she got up she found that father had lost all her money you left her. There was a dreadful scene between them. She told him he had robbed her and her child, and father left the house and swore he'd never come back again.

Sam. Don't be alarmed. He did come back.

Pol. Oh, yes. He was too good-hearted to stop away from his children long. He has his faults, but his good points, when you find them, are wonderful.

Sam. Yes, when you do find them.

Pol. So she had to come back here to us, and that's all.

Geo. Why didn't she write to my mother?

Pol. Father wanted her, but she was too proud. She said she'd die first.

Geo. (*rising; to* HAWTREE) There's a woman! Caste's all humbug! (*sees sword over mantlepiece*) That's my sword (*crosses* C., *round* R.) and a map of India—and that's the piano I bought her. I'll swear to the silk!

Pol. Yes, that was bought in at the sale.

Geo. (*to* HAWTREE) Thank you, old fellow.

Haw. Not by me. I was in India at the time.

Geo. By whom, then?

Pol. By Sam. (SAM *winks to her to discontinue*) I shall. He knew Esther was breaking her heart about anyone else having it, so he took the money he'd saved up for our wedding, and we're going to be married now, ain't we, Sam?   •

Sam. And hope by a constant attention to business to merit—— (POLLY *pushes him away*)

Pol. She's never touched the piano since you died ; but if I don't play to-night may I die an old maid. (*goes up and clears table*)

GEORGE *crosses to* SAM *and shakes his hand, then goes up stage, pulls up blind and looks into street—*SAM *finishes tea.*

Haw. (*aside*) Who'd have thought that little cad had it in him ! He never mentioned it. (*aloud*) Apropos, George, your mother. I'll go to the square, and tell her of—(*takes hat from piano*)

Geo. Is she in town ?

Haw. Yes. Will you come with me?

Geo. And leave my wife ! And such a wife !

Haw. I'll go at once. I shall catch her before dinner. Good-bye, old fellow ; seeing you back again alive and well, makes me feel quite—that I quite feel—(*shakes* GEORGE'S *hand, goes to door, then crosses to* SAM) Mr. Gerridge, I fear I have often made myself very offensive to you.

Sam. Well, sir, you have.

Haw. I feared so ; I didn't know you then ; I beg your pardon ; let me ask you to shake hands, forgive me and forget it. (*offering his hand*)

Sam. (*taking it*) Say no more, sir, and if ever I've made myself disagreeable to you, I ask your pardon, forget it and forgive me. (*they shake hands warmly*) And when you marry that young lady as I know you're engaged to, if you should furnish a house and require anything in my way—(*bringing out circular—*POLLY *comes down,* L., *and pushes him away ; he puts circular in his pocket and stands before fire*)

Haw. Good-bye, George, for the present. (*goes up*) Bye, Polly (*resumes his Pall Mall manner as he goes out*) I'm off to the square.

Exit, HAWTREE, R. D.

Geo. But Esther !

Pol. (*rising*) I'll tell her all about it.

Geo. How ?

Pol. I don't know ; but it will come. Providence will send it to me as it has sent you, my dear brother. You must go. (*crosses* C,) Esther will be getting up directly. (*at door,* GEORGE *looks through keyhole*) It's no use looking there ; it's dark.

Geo. (*at door*) It isn't often a man can see his own widow.

Pol. And it isn't often that he wants to. Now go away. (*pushing him off*)

Geo. I shall stop outside.

Sam. And I'll whistle for you when you may come in. (*crosses,* C.)

Pol. Now!

Geo. Oh! my Esther! When you know I'm alive I'll marry you. all over again, and have a second honeymoon! (*they force him off,* R. D.)

Pol. (*coming down*) Now, Sam, light the gas. I'm going to wake her up. Oh, my darling, if I dare tell you. (*whispering*) He's come back! He's come back! He's come back! Alive! Alive! Alive! Sam, kiss me! (*kisses* SAM *and goes off,* R. D.)

Sam. (*dances shutter dance*) I'm glad the swells are gone ; now I can open my safety valve and let my feelings escape. (*lights gas; stage light*) To think of his coming back alive from India, just as I'm going to open my shop. (*lights candles*) Perhaps he'll get me the patronage of the Royal Family. It'd look stunning over the door with a lion and a unicorn a-standing on their hind legs doing nothing furiously with a lozenge between them. (*sits on arm-chair,* R.) Poor Esther, to think of my knowing her when she was in the ballet line, then when she was in the honorable line, then a mother. No, honorables is mamma's. Then a widow and in the ballet line again. (*crosses,* L.) And him to come back (*growing affected*) and find a baby with all his furniture and fittings ready for immediate use. (*sits* L. *of table*) And the poor thing lying asleep with her eyelids hot and swollen—not knowing that that great, big, heavy, hulking, overgrown dragoon is prowling outside ready to fly at her lips, and strangle her in his strong loving arms. It—it—it——(*breaks down and sobs with his head upon the table*)

Enter, POLLY, *with a light colored dress on.*

Pol. Why, Sam, what's the matter?

Sam. (*rises and crosses,* R.) The water's got into my meter.

Pol. Hush!

Enter, ESTHER, R. D.; *they stop suddenly ;* POLLY *down stage.*

Sam. (*up stage, singing and dancing*) Tiddy-ti-tum-lo !

Est. (*sitting down near fire* L. *of head of table, taking up costume and beginning to work*) Sam, you seem in high spirits to-night.

Sam. (*crosses*) Yes ; you see Polly and I are going to be married, and, and hope by bestowing a favor to merit, to continuance, attention, by deserving a merit——

Pol. (*who has kissed* ESTHER *two or three times*) What are you talking about? (*comes down and sits on music stool*)

Sam. I don't know. I'm off my burner.

POLLY *goes round front of table to* L. C.

Est. What's the matter with you to-night, dear ? (*to* POLLY) I can see something in your eye.

Sam. It's the new furniture.

Pol. (*seated,* L. *of table*) It was a pretty dress when it was new ; not unlike the one Mdlle. Delphine used to wear. (*suddenly clapping her hands*) Oh !

Est. What's the matter ?

Pol. A needle ! (*aside to* SAM, *who crosses to her,* L.) I've got it.

Sam. The needle in your finger ?

Pol. No, an idea in my head.

Sam. (*still looking at finger*) Does it hurt ?

Pol. (*rises, crosses* C.) Stupid ! (SAM *crosses to* R. *again; aloud*) Do you recollect Mdlle. Delphine, Esther ?

Est. Yes.

Pol. Do you recollect her in that ballet that old Herr Griffenhaagen arranged—" Jeanne la Folle, or the Return of the Soldier?" (SAM *sits,* R. *on music stool*)

Est. Yes. Will you do the fresh hem ?

Pol. What's the use ? Let me see—how did it go ? How well I remember the scene. The cottage that side, the bridge at the back. La ! La ! La ! Ballet of villagers and the entrance of Delphine as Jeanne the bride. (*sings and pantomimes*) Then the entrance of Claude the bridegroom. Then there was the procession to church. The march of the soldiers over the bridge. (*sings and pantomimes*) Arrest of Claude, who is drawn for the conscription (*business ; and* ESTHER *looks dreamily*) and is torn from the arms of his bride at the church porch. Omnes broken-hearted ! This is Omnes broken-hearted. (*pantomimes*)

Est. Polly, I don't like this, it brings back memories.

Pol. (*going to table and leaning her hands on it looks over at* ESTHER) Oh ! fuss about memories. One can't mourn for ever. (ESTHER *surprised*) Everything in this world isn't sad. There's bad news, and—and, there's good news sometimes when we least expect it.

Est. Ah ! Not for me.

Pol. Why not ? (*pause ; crosses to* C.) Then the second act, you know—second act winter. (*taking chair to* R.) The village cross—this is the village cross. (*placing chair,* R.) Entrance of Jeanne—now called Jeanne la Folle, because she has gone mad. This is Jeanne gone mad. (*pantomimes*) Gone mad on account of the supposed loss of her husband.

Sam. The supposed loss ?

Pol. The supposed loss.

Est. (*dropping costume*) Polly !

Sam. Mind !

Pol. Mustn't stop now ; go on. Entrance of Claude, who isn't dead, in a captain's uniform—a cloak over his shoulder. Don't you recollect the ballet? Jeanne is mad and can't recognise her husband, and don't till he shows her the ribbon she gave him when they were betrothed. Here, I'll do it. I want a bit of ribbon. Sam, have you got a bit of ribbon? Ah! reach me that crape sword-knot, that will do. (*crosses*, R.; SAM *goes up*, L. C.)

Est. Touch that! (*rising and coming down*, L. C.)

Pol. Why not? It's no use now.

Est. You have heard of George! I know you have! I see it in your eyes! You may tell me! I can bear it! I can, indeed!—indeed I can! Tell me! He is not dead!

Pol. No!

Est.(*whispers*) Thank Heaven! Are you sure?

Pol. Quite.

Est. You've seen him! I see you have! I know it! I feel it! I had a bright and happy dream of him—I saw him as I slept. Oh! let me know if he is near! (*pacing stage*, L. *to* R.) Give me some sign, some sound—(POLLY *opens piano*) some token of his life and presence. (POLLY *whispers to* SAM *up* R. POLLY *plays piano on the treble only*—SAM *up by door*, R.)

Est. (*in an ecstacy*) O my husband! Come to me for I know that you are near! Let me feel your arms clasp round me! Do not fear for me! I can bear the sight of you! It will not kill me. George—love—husband—come! Oh, come to me! (*during this* GEORGE *has appeared at* R. D., *and running to* ESTHER *enfolds her in his embrace.* POLLY *plays the bass as well as treble of the air forte then fortissimo; she then plays at random, endeavoring to hide her tears—at last she strikes piano wildly, and goes off into a fit of hysterical laughter, to the alarm of* SAM, *who places her gently on the floor*—GEORGE *and* ESTHER *go up* C. *to cradle*)

Sam. Polly! Polly! my darling! (POLLY *seizes* SAM *by the hair and shakes him violently*)

Pol. Sam, Sam, I'm going mad!

Est. To see you here again, to feel your warm breath upon my cheek! Is it real? am I not dreaming? (*coming down*)

Sam. (L., *rubbing his head*) No, it's real.

Est. (*placing chair* C. *and kneeling on his left*) But tell us, tell us, do, darling, how you escaped.

Geo. It's a long story, but I'll condense it. I was riding out and suddenly found myself surrounded and taken prisoner. One of the troop that took me was a fella who had been my servant, and to whom I had done some little kindness; he helped me to escape and hid me in a sort of cave, and for a long time used to bring me food. Unfortunately, he was ordered away, so he brought another Sepoy to look after me. I felt from the first this man meant to betray me, and I watched him like a lynx during the one day he was with me. As evening drew on a Sepoy picket was passing; I could tell by the look in the fella's eyes he meant to call out as soon as they were near enough, so I seized him by the throat and shook the life out of him.

Est. (*standing over him*) You strangled him?

Geo. Yes.

Est. Killed him dead?

Geo. He didn't get up again.

Pol. (*to* SAM) You never go and kill Sepoys!

Sam. I pay rates and taxes.

Geo. The day after Havelock and his Scotchmen marched through the village, and I turned out to meet them. I was too done up to join, so I was sent straight on to Calcutta. I got leave, took a berth on the P. and O. boat—the passage restored me. I landed this morning, came on here and brought in the milk.

Enter, *the* MARQUISE, R. D.; *she rushes to embrace* GEORGE, C.

Mar. My dear boy! My dear, dear boy!

Pol. (*seated,* R.) Why, see, she's crying. She's glad to see him alive and back. (*goes up,* L.)

Sam. (*profoundly*) There's always something good in women, even when they're ladies. (*goes up.* POLLY *puts dress in box and goes to cradle*)

Mar. (*crosses to* ESTHER, L. C.). My dear daughter, we must forget our little differences. (*kissing her*) Won't you? How history repeats itself! You will find a similar and as unexpected a return mentioned by Froissart in the chapter that treats of Philip Dartnell.

Geo. Yes, mother. I remember. (*kisses her*)

Mar. (*to* GEORGE, *aside*) We'll take her abroad and make a lady of her.

Geo. Can't, mamma. She's ready made. Nature has done it to our hands.

Mar. (*aside to* GEORGE) But I won't have the man who smells of putty, nor the man who smells of beer. (*goes up and sits at fire*)

Enter, HAWTREE *very pale.*

Haw. George! Oh, the Marchioness is here.

Geo. What's the matter!

Haw. Oh, nothing. Yes, there is. I don't mind telling you. Why, I've been thrown. I called at my chambers as I came along and found this. (*gives* GEORGE *a note*)

Geo. From the Countess, Lady Florence, mother. (*reads*) " Dear Major Hawtree,—I hasten to inform you that my daughter, Florence, is about to enter upon an alliance with Lord Saxeby, the eldest son of the Marquis of Loamshire. Under these circumstances should you think fit to call here again I feel assured—"